James Davies

Fables

James Davies

Fables

ISBN/EAN: 9783744793834

Printed in Europe, USA, Canada, Australia, Japan

Cover: Foto ©Andreas Hilbeck / pixelio.de

More available books at **www.hansebooks.com**

THE
FABLES OF BABRIUS,

IN TWO PARTS.

TRANSLATED INTO ENGLISH VERSE

FROM THE TEXT OF SIR G. C. LEWIS.

BY THE

REV. JAMES DAVIES, M.A.
Sometime Scholar of Lincoln College, Oxford.

LONDON :
LOCKWOOD AND CO.
STATIONERS' HALL COURT.
MDCCCLX.

TO

THE RIGHT HONOURABLE

SIR GEORGE CORNEWALL LEWIS,

Secretary of State for the Home Department;
Honorary Student of Christ Church, Oxford, and
Editor of the Fables of Babrius,

THIS ATTEMPT TO RENDER INTO ENGLISH VERSE

THE FABLES OF AN AUTHOR,

WHOM HIS LITERARY LABOURS HAVE EFFECTUALLY

RESCUED FROM OBLIVION,

IS DEDICATED

WITH RESPECT AND GRATEFUL ACKNOWLEDGMENT

BY ONE

WHO WOULD FAIN TAKE HIM AS A MODEL

IN BLENDING CLASSICAL STUDY WITH THE SEVERER

DUTIES OF LIFE.

MOOR COURT, HEREFORDSHIRE,
June 27th, 1860.

PREFACE.

NO question is more often put to one who pro-
fesses an acquaintance with the Fables of Babrius
than, " Who was Babrius? when did he live?" and
the querist is sceptical, when, in answer, he is bidden
to discard, as erroneous, the notion that it is to Æsop,
and not to Babrius, that he owes the collection of
Fables which charmed his youth. Yet so it is, and
it is hoped that the version of Babrius into English,
now put forth, may, with the aid of a prefatory state-
ment, based on the researches of the learned, tend to
place the matter in a true light. Those who have no
knowledge of Classics will marvel to see how much
is owed to a fabulist, whose work has been rescued
from oblivion within the last twenty years.

Not that no traces, indeed, of Babrius existed before
that date. Bentley indicated remains of his Fables in

a dissertation which gave rise to the famous dispute respecting the Epistles of Phalaris. These traces, Tyrwhitt, in 1776, followed up, collecting all the fragments of Babrius found in the Grammarians, with some new verses from a MS. of Æsopian Fables in the Bodleian, and four entire fables (12, 58, 84, 129,) which had come down from one source or another. Later still, an Italian, Francesco de Furia, edited from MSS. in the Vatican library, several Fables before unpublished, which added greatly to the Babrian remains; for though in the form of prose, they were found easily reducible into Choliambic verse, into which they had been turned by our author from the oral or traditional collections of Æsopian Fables, and out of which (says Blomfield, Mus. Crit. 1. 410) they had been "transprosed" by some monk.[1]

---

[1] There seems to have been no written collection of Æsop; for when he is cited by ancient authors, there occurs a diversity which would have been prevented by a collected edition. See Smith's Dict. G. R. B. vol. i. p. 47, b. The same dictionary. ibid. has the following account of the spurious prose collections bearing the name of Æsop, now extant. "These are three. "One containing 136 Fables, published first A.D. 1610, from

In 1844, M. Minoides Menas, a learned Greek, commissioned by M. Villemain, Minister of Public Instruction under Louis Philippe, found, amongst other literary treasures, in the Convent of St. Laura, on Mount Athos, a MS. of Babrius, lost in the middle ages.[1] It was much damaged, and the monks asked so high a price for it, that Menas declined to buy it, and could only convey a transcript of it to Paris, which M. Villemain placed in the hands of M. Bois-

"MSS. at Heidelberg. This is so clumsy a forgery that it men-
"tions the orator Demades, who lived 200 years after Æsop,
"and contains a whole sentence from the Book of Job. Some
"of the passages Bentley has shown to be fragments of Choliam-
"bic verses, and has made it tolerably certain that they were
"stolen from Babrius. The second collection was made by a
"monk of Constantinople, Maximus Planudes, in the fourteenth
"century. These contain at least one Hebraism, and among
"them are words entirely modern, *e.g.* βούταλις, a bird,
"βούνευρον, a beast, and also traces of Babrius. The third col-
"lection was found in a MS. at Florence, and published in 1809.
"Its date is about a century before the time of Planudes, and it
"contains the life which was prefixed to his collection, and
"commonly thought to be his own."

[1] This MS., with another on paper, a transcript of one found a few years ago on Mount Athos, and containing 95 Fables, which appear as Part II. of the present translation, the Trustees of the British Museum purchased of M. Menas in 1857.

sonade (see Class. Mus. II. 413), by whom it was published in October, 1844. In this transcript and in the MS. the Fables are arranged alphabetically over eighty pages, according to the initial letter of each Fable, but the collection only reaches the letter O. The date of the MS. is supposed to be of the tenth century, from the peculiarities of writing observable in it. After several other continental editions[1] following closely on the Parisian, Sir G. C. Lewis, no new hand at Babrius even at that time (see a paper in Philol. Mus. I. p. 282), put forth the first edition of Babrius in England in 1846. This possesses among other advantages, that of entering the field late

---

[1] Boissonade's edition emends many blunders, which he ascribes to the Poet's being a Roman writing Greek, an idea which seems to be baseless. Many errors are probably referable to the transcriber. This first edition was followed very shortly by one from Berlin, by Lachmann and several distinguished coadjutors: an able work, enriched by a valuable appendix of Meineke on Choliambic metre, but unduly depreciatory of the previous labours of Boissonade. Soon after appeared an edition from the Zurich press, by Baiter and Orelli, printed in good type, and conveniently reserving for a subjoined "adnotatio critica" most of their conjectural emendations.

enough to have availed itself of whatever was valuable in the earlier editions. Its editor's Latin notes, concise and to the point, strike the scholar as the model of what Latin notes should be ; and afford an argument in favour of a practice falling into disuse and largely superseded by pages of English annotation, long drawn out, the quality of which is generally less remarkable than the quantity. Sir Cornewall's preface is exhaustive ; and to it, as well as to his supplementary MSS. notes, which, with other information, the translator is anxious to acknowledge with gratitude, the present preface is chiefly indebted for its materials.

The first important question suggested by Sir Cornewall's preface is as to the name and age of Babrius. He discards the notion of Boissonade that Babrius was a Roman,[1] one Valerius Babrius, observing that if he was, he was marvellously at

---

[1] This conjecture is based on the word Βαλεβρίου, in the MS. from Mount Athos, and on the title Βαλερίου χωριαμβικοὶ στίχοι prefixed to a fable "De Jove et Spe," in the Harl. MS. Both are corruptions of Βαβρίου.

home in Greek language and literature ; and at any rate was not desirous to pass for anything but a Greek. His knowledge of natural history, political institutions, mythology and geography, is all essentially Greek. He nowhere mentions Italy or Rome, or the lands to the west of the Mediterranean.

Assuming then that he was a Greek, we have but ,scanty data for a decision as to the time when he flourished. The notion in Tyrwhitt's day was that he lived at no long time prior to the Augustan age; a view which Sir G. C. Lewis seems to have held when he wrote a paper in the Philological Museum (I. p. 282), but which later studies have induced him to alter. The Swiss editors, from supposed traces of the Alexandrine grammarians and poets in his verse and diction, are inclined to fix his date about the time of Bion and Moschus ; while Bergk, in a paper in the Class. Museum (III. 130), places it as far back as B.C. 250, a time at which Alexander, son of Craterus, was ruler over Euboea and Corinth. Lachmann and Fixius each contend for other petty princes of a later date, in the Christian era. These are but a few guesses out of a number sufficient to justify the adaptation of an old proverb, " Quot critici, tot sententiæ ;" but Sir G. C. Lewis has relieved the question of a difficulty imported into it, by discrediting the hasty inference that the person addrest in Proem I, as ὦ Βράγχε τέκνον, is the same who in Proem II. is called ὦ παῖ βασιλέως 'Αλεξάνδρου. Attempts to fix what Alexander is meant, by connecting him with a son named Branchus, may well be deemed labour lost.[1] The natural inference is that in the First Proem, and elsewhere, Branchus, a son of the poet, is addressed, and that for his instruction the Fables were written ; but that the Second Proem of Part I. which was prefixed probably to a second edition, so to speak, of the whole Fables, was dedicated to a son of some prince or Emperor Alexander, to whom Babrius looked up as his patron.

Sir G. C. Lewis favours the opinion of Boissonade

[1] See Proem I. v. 1. Part 1st ; Proem II. v. 1. Part 1st. And compare with these the Proem commencing the Second Part of the Fables, which begins ἄκουσον, ὦ παῖ ; and also Fab. xxiv. v. 19. Part II.

that this Alexander was Alexander Severus (the date of whose death was A.D. 235), and as this is only conjecture, he brings in support of it several corroborative circumstances, which tend greatly to establish a probability.

In the first place, Babrius is cited by no earlier writer than Dositheus Magister,[1] a grammarian, who lived about 207 A.D., and in whose 'Ερμηνεύματα are two Fables of Babrius in Choliambic verse (F. 84, 129); which, if Dositheus himself introduced into his own work, will bring Babrius to a date not later than Septimius Severus, A.D. 207, or his son, Caracalla, to whom Alexander Severus claimed sonship.

Again we may refer the words of Babrius in Proem II. Part I. (where the Poet traces the origin

---

[1] Plutarch, Lucian, Athenæus, are silent as to Babrius; yet, had Babrius lived prior to the time of Augustus, some of his fables would probably have found their way into Plutarch : but when that writer does introduce fables of a common subject with those of Babrius, he invariably follows another version. Phædrus, too, boasting to be the first to transplant Greek fable into Latium, mentions Æsop alone, as furnishing his materials. It would follow that Babrius was unknown to Phædrus, and Phædrus probably lived in the time of Tiberius.

of the " Fable" to Syria Antiqua, a view held by no
other Greek writer), to a wish to flatter his assumed
patron, Alexander Severus, who was born in Phœ-
nicia. It is clear, too, that the Poet had some Asiatic
connexion,[1] which might still farther account for his
desire to please this prince, who was, moreover, an
especial patron and student of Greek literature ;[2] nor
need it be any stumbling-block that this Alexander is
termed Βασιλεύς, seeing that Roman princes were so
called by the Greeks.

Those who are dissatisfied with this attempt to fix
the date of Babrius, will find no traces of his Fables
earlier than the Emperor Julian, a century or more
later ; who, in his Epistle LIX, quotes a verse of
the thirty-second Fable, v. 1. without the author's
name. Tzetzes and Suidas, alone, the latest of the
grammarians, quote much from Babrius, previous to
the finding of the present MSS.; and all that we can

---

[1] Thus he was familiar with the Arabs, Fab. 57, v. 12. The
name, too, Branchus, indicates a connexion with Asia. So too,
perhaps, does the dialect he uses, *i.e.* the Ionic. (See below.)

[2] See Lamprid. vit. Alex. Sev. c. 27, 30.

arrive at, with any approximation to certainty, is, that
Babrius lived between the close of the first century
after Christ and the age of Julian.

There was no Greek metrical version of the
Æsopian Fables before that of Babrius. Socrates
seems to have versified a Fable or two in elegiacs
whilst in prison. Demetrius Phalereus published
a collection, but that was in prose. When fables
occur in Xenophon, Aristotle, Plutarch, and Lucian,
they are narrated in the writer's own words, not cited
from any poet. Suidas gives fragments of fables in
Elegiac or Heroic verse, but whence gathered is unknown. Callimachus would seem to have turned
some Æsopian Fables into Choliambics ; but Babrius
claims the honour to himself, and says (Proem II.
9—12) that many imitators forthwith sprung up. His
Fables were known in Greece before the age of Suidas
and Tzetzes : and the prose collections of Maximus
Planudes, and others in later days, have been mainly
based on his version. Nor was it till after the revival
of letters that the opinion obtained any credence,
that the prose Æsopian Fables were really those of

Æsop. Nothing could be more manifestly unsound.
Even before Bentley, learned men pronounced them
the offspring of later monks : not probably designed
to be literary impostures, but rather entertaining
paraphrases. In any wise the Fables of Babrius may
claim to be the basis, or stock material, of all that
comes down to our day under the name and credit
of Æsop.

The nature of the present work, intended as it is
for the general reader, precludes any extended remarks upon the Choliambic Metre, in which the
Fables of Babrius are written. Scholars will find
the subject amply treated in the preface of Sir G. C.
Lewis (pp. xv—xx). Suffice it here to say that a
Choliambic (a lame, halt Iambic) differs from the
Iambic Senarius in always having a spondee or
trochee for its last foot : the fifth foot, to avoid slow-
ness of metre, being generally an Iambic.

Neither need more be said respecting the dialect
of Babrius than that it is Ionic, but with great ap-
proaches to the Attic dialect in later and more common use. The Ionic was the dialect used by all

b

Choliambic poets from the days of Hipponax and Ananius,[1] and it was therefore natural that Babrius should follow it, even if not, as seems possible, himself connected with Ionia.

A very interesting portion of Sir G. C. Lewis's preface is his analysis of the Æsopian Fable, with a view to establishing the indigenous Greek origin of this class of compositions from a consideration of its natural history.

It seems to have been the peculiarity of the Æsopian Fable to admit sometimes mere apologues (*e.g.* F. ii. xv.), sometimes conversations between gods and men (*e.g.* x. xx. xxx.); but chiefly to introduce brutes, or inanimate nature, as endowed with speech, for the inculcation of virtue, prudence, or political truth.[2]

---

[1] Hipponax was an Ionian, who flourished B.C. 540, and Ananius about the same period. See an account of them in Muller and Donaldson's Hist. Gr. Lit. vol. i. pp. 188—91.

[2] "In the Æsopean Fable the actions and business of men are the real and prominent object, while beasts are merely introduced as a veil or disguise. It is exclusively the invention of those who detected in the social habits of the lower animals points

In Babrius, the chief interlocutors are the Lion and the Fox, especially the former,[1] who figures as the king of beasts with royal title and prerogatives. And there is abundant proof that the lion was in the earliest ages a native of the Peloponese as well as of Northern Greece. The tiger never appears as a character in Æsopian Fable, though incidentally mentioned once or twice by Babrius. (P. I. Fab. xcv. 17—19; cii. 7—9.) It was unknown in Greece until after the expedition of Alexander. The most ancient fable in which it is found bearing a part is that of Avianus (Fab. 17) in the fifth century. The spotted pard, which occurs once in Part II. lxxii. and incidentally in

of resemblance with those of man ; and while they retained their real character in some respects, found means, by the introduction of reason and speech, to place them in the light required for their purpose."—*Muller and Donaldson's Gr. Lit.* vol. i. 192.

[1] A strong argument against the Roman origin of Babrius. There is no reason to believe that the lion ever existed in Italy, except when in the Imperial period he was imported from Africa for the combats of the Amphitheatre. See "Lion in Greece," G. C. L. Notes and Queries, Vol. viii. p. 81, 2d Series. "Lion in Italy," Ibid. p. 282. See also the Preface to Babrius, pp. xxii. xxiii.

Part I. (Fab. cii. 8), is mentioned in Homer, and
is a native of Arabia and Palestine. There seems
to have been, even in later times, a constant confusion between the tiger and the leopard.

Besides the domestic animals (the horse, ass, ox,
goat, sheep, dog, and cat[1]), we find the wolf and
the stag, and occasionally the bear, introduced into
these fables. The camel and the ape[2] appear
more rarely, and the sow, as an unclean beast,
more rarely still. There are two instances of its
introduction in the recently discovered portion of
Babrius. (Cf. Part II. Fab. lxxiv. lxxv.) The
elephant also only finds a place in Fable xli. of

---

[1] The ancients did not distinguish accurately between αἴλουρος,
"the cat," and γαλῆ, "the weasel." Cf. Fab. xvii. xxvii. xxxi.
xxxii. cxxi.; Part II. Fab. lxvii. The same confusion occurs in
Latin between "mustela" and "feles." Both animals appear
to have been kept by the ancients for the same object, to kill
birds and mice. See Notes and Queries, 2d Series, Vol. viii.
p. 261, &c. "Ancient Names of the Cat."

[2] The Camel, Part I. xl. lxxx.; Part II. lxxvii. The Ape,
Part I. xxxv. lvi.; Part II. xxiii. and lxxviii. In the second
part we find the hedgehog, lxxiii., the flea in Fab. xcii. xciii.
xciv., and even a more unpresentable insect is mentioned in
Fab. lxxxvi.

the second part. The cock, however, plays a very conspicuous part in the Æsopian Fable. (Cf. v. xvii. cxxi. cxxiii.; Part II. xvi.) This bird was a very early importation from Asia into Greece, though after the time of Homer. (Cf. Knight's Proleg. to Hom. § 6.)

On the whole, it may be affirmed that though Babrius occasionally mentions animals of foreign extraction, and known only to the later Greeks, yet he only or chiefly introduces those, as characters in his Fables, which are recognised by the earliest traditions of the Æsopian Fables : a strong argument for the European origin of this class of fiction.

The style of Babrius is justly described as easy, pure, and elegant. Neither, while it is far from being ornate, is it in any degree bald or meagre. He seems to have aimed at that simplicity and clearness which are most essential to the force and point of fable-literature. His plots are, generally, versified forms of the oral or traditional collections, purporting to be those of Æsop. But he here and there apparently introduces some of his own invention, or some which are adapted from others. His epimyth, or moral, constantly differs from that of the parallel prose fable which has come down to us; a remark which suggests the question of the genuineness of these epimyths : into which, as regards Part I, Sir G. C. Lewis has carefully examined, in some MSS. notes, which he has kindly communicated to the translator—the results of which are subjoined.[1]

It now remains that some notice should be taken of the second part of Babrius, edited in 1859 by Sir G. C. Lewis, from a transcript by M. Menas of a MS. on Mount Athos ; which, with the original of

[1] He divides the epimyths of Part I. into three classes, the spurious, the doubtful, and the genuine, as follows :—

Spurious. Fab. xiii. xxix. (v. 5) xxxiii. xxxviii. lii. lx. lxxi. lxxii. lxxxii. lxxxiv. lxxxv. (v. 20) xciv. (v. 10) xcvi. cvii. cxxix.

Doubtful. Fab. xxi. xxiv. xxv. xliii. lvi. lxxxi. lxxxiii.

Genuine. Fab. iv. v. ix. x. xi. xii. xiv. xviii. xxii. (v. 15) xxiii. xxix. (v. 6,) xxxi. xxxiv. xxxv. xxxvi. xl. xli. xliv. xlvii. l. lix. lxiv. lxv. lxvi. lxvii. lxx. lxxiv. lxxxv. (v. 19) xciv. (v. 9) cxvi.

In translation, these have generally been rendered, except in one or two instances, where it was difficult to make any sense of what was evidently spurious. It would not be difficult to arrange, under the three classes above, the epimyths of the second part.

the copy from which the Parisian edition of 1844 was printed, was purchased by the Trustees of the British Museum, in 1857. It has come to us in a very imperfect state, and far removed from its pristine form, both as to metre and diction. Yet ample marks and traces of Babrius remain in both respects, traces which could not be the result of literary fraud. It appears that at first there was considerable suspicion of forgery with reference to this MS. But in the words of Sir G. C. Lewis, "the undesigned " coincidences with the prose Fables are beyond the " skill of any forger." " I have no doubt" (he adds) "that the MS. of Menas was what it professed to " be, namely, a copy from a genuine archetype." Such is also the opinion of other scholars who at first doubted ; and it is one which a comparison of the recovered Fables with the corresponding prose versions will certainly strengthen and confirm.

The second part of Babrius is edited by our English Editor, more briefly than the first. And there are very many sentences in its text, which critical skill can hardly remedy. To translate such is, perhaps, a matter of ingenuity, of which the translator trusts that he has not entirely fallen short ; though once or twice he has been obliged to omit a passage, of which he could make literally nothing.

In both parts his great aim has been to produce a version which, while literal, should preserve, as far as lay in his power, the elegance and terseness of the original : a difficult task, in which he can at most hope to have achieved but partial success. It would be ungrateful, before committing the volume to the public, to omit testifying to the ready assistance and kindly encouragement to persevere in a work, in some slight degree akin to his own, which he has received throughout from the distinguished scholar and statesman, who, among other titles, may claim that of being the English editor of Babrius.

INDEX.

PART I.

PART II.

FABLES OF BABRIUS.

PROEM I.

THE race of just men flourish'd first, of old ;
    Its name, son Branchus, was the " age of gold."

       *   *   *   *   *

Third after these was born a brazen race,
And next the god-sprung heroes found their place :
Fifth came a stock depraved, an iron root.
But 'twas the Golden age, when every brute
Had voice articulate, in speech was skill'd,
And the mid-forests with its synods fill'd.
The tongues of rock and pine-leaf then were free ;
To ship and sailor then would speak the sea ;
Sparrows with farmers would shrewd talk maintain :
Earth gave all fruits, nor ask'd for toil again.
Mortals and gods were wont to mix as friends.
To which conclusion all the teaching tends
Of sage old Æsop ; him, to whom belong
Fables set forth in free, outspoken song.
These should a place in thy remembrance get ;
Therefore for thee this honeycomb I set,
Desirous, as I hive it, to assuage
The harsh Iambic's bitterness and rage.

PROEM II.

The Fable, royal Alexander's son !
Is a device by Syrians old begun.
Belus and Ninus ruled, when it was young.
And clever Æsop to th' Hellenic tongue
Gave fables first.   The like Cybisas spake
To Libyans.   I, in mine, old forms forsake,
And, with gold cheek-piece bitting fiery horse,
Commend my mythiambic to the course.
Yet I no sooner had unbarr'd the door,
Than others enter'd.   Theirs the Muse to soar
In griffin-like productions, over-wise ;
Tho' past mine own their knowledge doth not rise.
Now I in simple speech my fables set,
Nor care the famed Iambic's teeth to whet.
Rather to dull their edge, to soothe their stings,
Aims he, who now this second volume sings.

FABLE I.

THE ARCHER AND THE LION.
(P. F. 403.)

A SKILFUL archer the hill country sought,

Intent on sport.   His coming quickly brought

To every wild beast fear and headlong flight.

The lion only tarried to invite

The archer's onslaught. " Haste not ! Prythee stay,"

The stranger said ; " nor hope to win the day.

" Learn from mine envoy, whom you soon shall meet.

" Your wisest plan."   Forth sped his arrow fleet

From no great distance ; and was buried deep

In the beast's flank.   Afraid his post to keep

The wounded lion straight essay'd to fly

To where the lonesome woodland thickets lie.

But, lo ! a fox was standing at his side,

Who urg'd him still the archer's shafts to bide.

" Not so !" the lion said ; " beguile not me !

" Yon envoy came but now so bitterly,

" That doubly fierce his master needs must be."

II.

THE HUSBANDMAN WHO HAD LOST HIS MATTOCK.

TRENCHING his vineyard once a husbandman
His mattock lost ; and to inquire began,
If it had gone by any workman's theft.
But each denied.   When no resource was left,
To put them on their oaths, he took them all
Up to the city.   'Tis our wont to call
The country gods poor folks : but those who dwell
In walls, we deem, are true, and order well.
Now in a fountain in the foregate street
The party stay'd to rest, and wash'd their feet.
Just then the crier rich rewards was telling
To him who'd show who robb'd the sacred dwelling.
The farmer heard, and said, " My journey's vain !
" If the god knows not, who has robbed his fane,
" And but from men, for bribes, the news receives,
" How can he know, or find out, other thieves ? "

III.

THE GOATHERD AND THE SHE GOAT.
(P. F. 17.)

A GOATHERD wish'd to gather home his flock ;
Some came : some tarried ; on a cleft of rock
The fragrant shoots of mastich and goatsrue
One she-goat into disobedience drew.
Quickly the hireling lifted up a stone,
Which brake her horn, tho' from a distance thrown.
And now he sued her : " Goat and fellow-slave,
" By Pan, the patron of these glens, I crave,
" Do not thou to my lord this act proclaim,
" I meant not that the stone should take good aim."
" Nay, how," said she, " a plain fact can I hide ?
" My horn is telltale, tho' my tongue be tied."

IV.

THE FISHERMAN AND THE FISH.
(P. F. 26.)

His late-cast net ashore a fisher drew,
Enclosing fish, not all alike nor few ;
The smaller, taking flight, contrived to get
Safe through the bottom of the meshy net,
Whilst in the ship the greater emptied lay.

'Tis surely safe, and farthest from harm's way,
To be but small : for you shall seldom see
The high in rank escape calamity.

V.

THE YOUNG COCKS.
(P. F. 21.)

Two Tanagræan cocks a fight began ;
Their spirit is, 'tis said, as that of man ;
Of these the beaten bird, a mass of blows,
For shame into a corner creeping goes ;

The other to the housetop quickly flew,

And there in triumph flapp'd his wings, and crew.

But him an eagle lifted from the roof,

And bore away.   His fellow gain'd a proof

That oft the wages of defeat are best,

None else remain'd the hens to interest.

Wherefore, O man, beware of boastfulness, ⎫

Should fortune lift thee, others to depress, ⎬

Many are saved by lack of her caress. ⎭

VI.

THE FISHERMAN AND THE LITTLE FISH.
(P. F. 28.)

A FISHERMAN, who all the seashore drain'd,

While he with slender rod sweet life maintain'd,

Once caught with horsehair line a tiny fish,

Ill-suited for the frying-pan or dish.

The gasping fish its captor thus besought :

" What am I worth ? For what shall I be bought ?

" I'm not half-grown ! whom on yon rocky shore

" My mother in the sea-weed lately bore.

" Now let me go ; oh, kill me not in vain,

" And you shall catch me when you come again,

" On sea-weed food ere then grown large and fine,

" And meet to grace a board, where rich men dine."

As thus she prayed, she raised a piteous moan

And panted much ; but the old man was stone.

Vain was her hope with winning words to plead ;

He said, while piercing her with ruthless reed :

" Who holds not fast a small but certain prize,

" Is but a fool, to seek uncertainties."

VII.

THE HORSE AND THE ASS.
(P. F. 177.)

A MAN, who kept a horse, along the way

Unladen used to lead him, and to lay

His burden on an aged ass, who groaned,

And coming to the horse his fate bemoaned.

" Wouldst thou but share my load, I might survive,"

Said he, " but else I sha'n't be long alive."

" Move on," the other cried ; " don't worry me !"

The ass crept on reproved ; and presently

Sank under toil, and died as he had said ;

His master therefore set the horse instead

Beside him, shifted all the weight, and laid

This and the ass's skin, when it was flay'd,

With all its trappings, on the horse's back :

He cried, " Ah, ill advised ! alack, alack !

" I would not bear a part, however small ;

" And now constraint hath laid upon me all."

VIII.

THE ARAB AND THE CAMEL.
(P. F. 68.)

An Arab, having heap'd his camel's back,

Ask'd if he chose to take the upward track

Or downward ; and the beast had sense to say,

" Am I cut off then from the level way ? "

IX.

THE FISHERMAN PIPING.

(Γ. F. 27.)

A FISHER play'd the pipes with wondrous skill,
And hoping shoals of fish, of their own will,
Would to the sweet sound of his piping throng,
Let down his net, and piped a tuneful song.
But when his breath was spent, his piping nought,
He cast again, and fish in numbers caught.
These panting here and there ashore he spied,
And, as he wash'd his net, thus sharply cried :
" Dance without music now ! Had ye been wise,
" Ye had before danced to my melodies."

Indifference is oft a losing game ;
But when you catch the prize, at which you aim,
Then is your time to ridicule and blame.

X.

THE FEMALE SLAVE AND VENUS.

A MAN, enamour'd of his ugly slave,

An arrant slut, to her for asking gave

Whate'er she would. Hence, as more gauds she wins,

And trails fine purple o'er her slattern shins,

At wife and mistress she defiance flings ;

But Venus, as the cause of these good things,

With lamps she fain would honour, and each day

Make offering, supplicate, pay vows, and pray ;

Till to her came the goddess, in her sleep,

And, while the house was hush'd in slumber deep,

Said, " Thank me not, as tho' I'd made thee fair ;

" To him that thinks thee so, a hate I bear."

Whoso in what is foul can beauty find,

Is surely God-abhorr'd, and halt in mind.

XI.

THE MAN AND THE FOX.
(P. F. 61.)

A MAN, that on his vines' and orchards' foe,
The fox, a strange affront design'd to throw,
Bandag'd its tail with tow, applied a light,
And sent it forth.   Now Heaven's just oversight
Led the flame-bearer to its captor's fields ;
It was the time for crops, when harvest yields
A hopeful prospect of abundant share ;
The man pursued, deploring wasted care ;
And Ceres did not bless his threshing-floor.

One should be meek, and ne'er be vexèd sore.
Anger a vengeance worth avoidance hath,
That bringeth damage to the quick-to-wrath.

XII.

THE NIGHTINGALE AND THE SWALLOW.
(P. F. 10.)

FAR from men's fields the swallow forth had flown,

When she espied amid the woodlands lone

The nightingale, sweet songstress.   Her lament

Was Itys to his doom untimely sent.

Each knew the other through the mournful strain,

Flew to embrace, and in sweet talk remain.

Then said the swallow, " Dearest, liv'st thou still ?

" Ne'er have I seen thee, since thy Thracian ill.

" Some cruel fate hath ever come between ;

" Our virgin lives till now apart have been.

" Come to the fields : revisit homes of men :

" Come dwell with me, a comrade dear, again,

" Where thou shalt charm the swains, no savage brood :

" Dwell near men's haunts, and quit the open wood :

" One roof, one chamber, sure, can house the two,

" Or dost prefer the nightly frozen dew,

" And day-god's heat ? a wild-wood life and drear ?

" Come, clever songstress, to the light more near."

To whom the sweet-voiced nightingale replied :

" Still on these lonesome ridges let me bide ;

" Nor seek to part me from the mountain glen ;

" I shun, since Athens, man, and haunts of men ;

" To mix with them, their dwelling place to view,

" Stirs up old grief, and opens woes anew."

Some consolation for an evil lot

Lies in wise words, in song, in crowds forgot.

But sore the pang, when, where you once were great,

Again men see you, housed in mean estate.

XIII.

THE HUSBANDMAN AND THE STORK.
(P. F. 100.)

THIN nets a farmer o'er his furrows spread,

And caught the cranes that on his tillage fed :

And him a limping stork began to pray,

Who fell with them into the farmer's way :

" I am no crane : I don't consume the grain :

" That I'm a stork is from my colour plain ;

" A stork, than which no better bird doth live :

" I to my father aid and succour give."

The man replied : " Good stork, I cannot tell

" Your ways of life : but this I know full well,

" I caught you with the spoilers of my seed :

" With them, with whom I found you, you must bleed."

Walk with the bad, and hate will be as strong

'Gainst you as them, e'en though you no man wrong.

XIV.

THE BEAR AND THE FOX.

(P. F. 69.)

A BEAR for man was boasting fondness rare,

Whose corpse, he urged, he was not wont to tear.

To whom quoth Reynard, " Were the choice my
   own,

" You should tear corpses, but let life alone ;

" Let none that hurt my life, my death bemoan."

C

XV.

THE ATHENIAN AND THE THEBAN.
(P. F. 50.)

A THEBAN and Athenian took one road,
And thence, no marvel, conversation flow'd.
They came to speak of heroes, in their walk,
And, after other long and needless talk,
The Theban fain Alcmena's son would prove
Greatest of men, and now of gods above.
Th' Athenian argued, that far nobler fate
Was that of Theseus, so divine his state,
Compared with Herc'les and his servile lot :
And soon the wordy talker victory got.
The other, Theban-like, in words outmatch'd,
Thus, with rough wit, the argument despatch'd :
" There : you prevail ! So then may we displease
" Theseus : and you Athenians Hercules !"

XVI.

THE WOLF AND THE NURSE.
(P. F. 275.)

A COUNTRY nurse, to fright her babe to peace,
Said, " Wolf shall have thee, or thy cries must cease."
The wolf o'erheard, believed the scolding crone,
And stay'd in hopes to find the feast his own.
But evening came ; the babe was hush'd to rest :
The wolf still gaped, with rav'ning hunger prest.
At last his hopes to utter dulness grew :
Then to his anxious helpmate he withdrew.
" How cam'st thou empty ?" said she.   He replied,
" Because upon a female I relied."

XVII.

THE CAT AND THE COCK.
(P. F. 15.)

A CAT that ambush'd for some house-birds lay,
Swung itself, baglike, from a peg one day.
'Twas seen by a sagacious shrewd-tongued cock,
Which shrilly thus began the cat to mock ;
" Full many bags I've noticed heretofore :
" But none the grinders of a live cat bore."

XVIII.

THE NORTH WIND AND THE SUN.
(P. F. 82.)

BETWIXT the North wind and the Sun arose
A contest, which would soonest of his clothes
Strip a wayfaring clown, so runs the tale.
First Boreas blows an almost Thracian gale,
Thinking perforce to steal the man's capote :
He loos'd it not : but as the cold wind smote

More sharply, tighter round him drew the folds,
And sheltered by a crag his station holds.
But now the Sun at first peer'd gently forth,
And thaw'd the chills of the uncanny north ;
Then in their turn his beams more amply plied,
Till sudden heat the clown's endurance tried :
Stripping himself, away his cloak he flung :
The Sun from Boreas thus a triumph wrung.

The fable means, " My son, at mildness aim :
Persuasion more results than force may claim."

XIX.

THE FOX AND THE GRAPES.
(P. F. 33.)

THERE hung some bunches of the purple grape
On a hill-side. A cunning fox, agape
For these full clusters, many times essay'd
To cull their dark bloom, many vain leaps made.

They were quite ripe, and for the vintage fit :
But when his leaps did not avail a whit,
He journey'd on, and thus his grief composed :
" The bunch was sour, not ripe, as I supposed."

XX.

THE CARTER AND HERCULES.
(P. F. 81.)

A CARTER from the village drove his wain :
And when it fell into a rugged lane,
Inactive stood, nor lent a helping hand ;
But to that God, whom of the heavenly band
He really honour'd most, Alcides, pray'd :
" Push at your wheels," the God appearing said,
" And goad your team ; but, when you pray again,
" Help yourself likewise, or you'll pray in vain."

XXI.

THE OXEN AND THE BUTCHERS.
(P. F. 80.)

SOME oxen wish'd the butcher tribe to kill,
Who boasted a to them destructive skill.
But when they met, and now for direful fray
Whetted their horns, an ox of ancient day
Among them, who for years had borne the plough,
Said, " These at least have hands experienced, how
" To kill and carve us, not to hack and hew :
" But if we chance on men to slaughter new,
" We shall die twice.   One will not lack to fell
" The ox, but one perhaps to do it well."

A man in haste from present woes to flee
Should see his path from worse disaster free.

XXII.

THE GRIZZLED MAN AND HIS TWO SWEET-HEARTS.
(P. F. 56.)

A MAN on whom mid-age its mark had set,—
He was no longer young, nor old as yet,—
Was wont to brush his black hair mixt with grey.
And then in Love's sweet revels spend his day.
He wooed two loves, a young one and an old ;
The young one was desirous to behold
Her lover youthful.   Age would mate with age.
Hence evermore the damsel strove to wage
War against each grey hair she chanc'd to find :
The elder tried to leave no black behind ;
Till each in turn, by plucking out his hair,
Young love and old, had left him bald and bare.

Woe worth the man entrapp'd by woman's lure,
For such are ever pluck'd and stripp'd, be sure.

XXIII.

THE DROVER THAT LOST A BULL.
(P. F. 83.)

To a far forest for a bull that stray'd,
A well-horn'd beast, a drover quest had made.
Then to the mountain nymphs and gods around,
Hermes and Pan, he sware, in case he found
The thief, a lamb should fall a sacrifice.
Crossing a hill, his noble bull he spies
Feasting a lion.   Then he vows in grief,
To add an ox, if he escape the thief.

Hence, it would seem, this lesson we are taught,
Not to uplift a vow devoid of thought,
By instant trouble's pressure overwrought.

XXIV.

THE MARRIAGE OF THE SUN.
(P. F. 77.)

THE Sun's espousals were at summer's prime,
Hence all the beasts enjoy'd a jovial time.
The frogs too led the dance in marsh and mere,
Till a toad check'd them, saying, " Nought is here
" To call for joy, but rather grief and moan,
" For if he dries each spring, while yet alone,
" How by this union are we not undone,
" If like himself he should beget a son ? "

Many o'er trifles needlessly exult,
From which too often sorrow will result.

XXV.

THE HARES AND THE FROGS.
(P. F. 237.)

To end their days the hares made up their mind,

And since they were of beasts the feeblest kind,

Timid of heart, and dull in all but flight,

To hide themselves in some dark pool from light.

But as to a broad swamp they drew more near,

Upon its margin hosts of frogs appear,

Which into slimy depths affrighted leap.

As the hares paused, one said, " Your courage keep.

" Let us return ! To die we need not seek,

" For here are others than ourselves more weak."

XXVI.

THE FARMER AND THE CRANES.
(P. F. 93.)

A FARMER'S land, fresh sown with wheaten grain,

Was being wasted by the hurtful crane.

Long did the farmer lift an empty sling,

By fear alone their troop discomfiting.

But when they found he only smote the air,

To fly at his approach they did not care :

Till he no longer made a feint to throw,

But laid with stones the greater number low.

Quitting the corn, the rest began to cry,

" Come, to the land of pygmies let us fly.

" This man, it seems, content no more with fright,

" Is now beginning to put forth his might."

XXVII.

THE CAPTURED WEASEL.
(P. F. 89.)

A MAN had trapp'd a weasel, which to drown,
He in a water-vessel tied it down.
But when she said, "How shamefully my aid
In catching mice and lizards have you paid!"
"I own the debt," cried he; "but did not you
"Stifle each bird, and rob each dwelling too,
"And empty every meat-pot? You shall die!
"For I'm more hurt than profited thereby."

XXVIII.

THE OX AND THE TOAD.
(P. F. 84.)

AN ox at water once a toadling crush'd,
Whose dam, then absent, quickly homeward rush'd,
And question'd all its brethren where it was:
"Mother, 'tis dead. Before its time, alas,

" Beneath the hoof of a huge quadruped

" 'Twas trampled down !" " Was it as large," she said,

" As this ? " She tried her proper size to strain.

" Mother," cried they, " forbear ! nor fume in vain.

" You'll rend yourself in sunder, ere you rise,

" Howe er you ape it, to that monster's size."

XXIX.

THE AGED HORSE.
(P. F. 174.)

ONCE an old horse was sold to work the mill :

And yok'd each eve a grinder's task to fill.

At last it groan'd and said : " What courses past,

" Round what strange millers' turns I wheel at last !"

Be not too much with fortune's hopes elate :

Age ends for many in a troubled state.

XXX.

THE SCULPTOR AND MERCURY.
(P. F. 26₅.)

A MAN had wrought a Mercury for sale
In marble.   Would-be buyers did not fail.
One for a pillar (he'd just lost a son)
To buy it wish'd, for a god's statue one.
Night came : yet it the sculptor had not sold,
So he agreed at morn again t' unfold
The statue, if they'd come.   In slumber deep
He gazed on Hermes at the gates of sleep,
Who said, " Good measure of my worth you take,
" Since god or corpse of me you mean to make."

XXXI.

THE CATS AND MICE.
(P. F. 291.)

BETWEEN the cats and mice of old there raged
A truceless war : a feud no blood assuaged.
The cats were victors.   And the vanquished mice
Deem'd this the cause, and this their army's vice,

A lack of leaders of distinguisht front,
And discipline, to meet the battle's brunt.
Then chose they mice for rank, might, counsel, famed,
And, as to prowess, more than all unblamed.
Who marshalling their squadrons soon devise
A mimic phalanx, troops, and companies.
Now, all array'd and marshall'd, forth there stood
A mouse, and challenged all the feline brood.
Thin straws from mud walls every chief had bound
Before his brows.   Beheld of all around,
They took the lead, the foremost of the host :
Alas ! again the mice the day have lost.
Safe to their holes the undistinguish'd fled :
But for each vainly-ornamented head
The narrow entrance proved, alack, too small :
Alone outside were ta'en the heroes all.
Meetly o'er them the foe a trophy set :
For each mouse-chief a feline captor met.

Our fable's moral is, that safety lies
Less in high rank than that which most despise.

XXXII.

THE CAT AND VENUS.
(P. F. 88.),

A CAT, that loved a handsome man, was blest

By the Loves' mother granting her request :

To change her shape permission Venus gave

For lovely woman's : such who would not rave

Unless he won ?   'Twas now the man's to bend

To love and marriage.   At the banquet's end

A mouse ran past.   Down the deep couch's side

Intent upon its capture sprang the bride.

The nuptials ceased.   Love vanish'd from among

His mocking sports.   For nature was too strong.

XXXIII.

THE FARMER AND THE STARLINGS.
(P. F. 99.)

THE Pleiads set, 'twas time to cast the seed :

A farmer sow'd his fallow : then took heed

To watch and guard it ; for a countless host

Of black and croaking daws had o'er it cross'd,

D

And starlings, bent the tillage to destroy.

With empty sling there follow'd him a boy.

Now with the starlings 'twas the usual thing,

To list the farmer calling for his sling ;

And fly ere he discharged it.　Hence he sought

A new device, and thus the stripling taught

To act.　" My lad, since we must needs outwit

" This clever race of birds, a plan I've hit.

" So when they come, and I for bread shall ask,

" To hand the sling, not bread, will be your task."

The starlings came, and on the tillage fed ;

And he, as was agreed on, ask'd for bread.

They did not fly.　The lad supplied the stones

And sling.　The old man aim'd and brake the bones

Of many a starling : shoulders, crowns, and shins :

Till from his land the remnant flight begins.

Some cranes that met them ask'd them " how they
　　fare ? "

Then said a daw : " Of base mankind beware !

" Each speaks to other, words unlike his deeds."

Dread is the race that but by guile succeeds.

XXXIV.

THE BOY EATING THE ENTRAILS.
(P. F. 348.)

WHAT time with vineboughs men the broad-floor strew,

A bull to Ceres once the rustics·slew.

Tables of meat and casks of wine were there ;

But one poor lad had gorged too large a share

Of the bull's entrails.   Swoln he homeward hies,

And sore bewails his stomach's weight and size.

Once in his mother's arms, "Alas !" cried he.

"What is't ?" she said.   "Oh, all is o'er with me !

" My wretched fate is present death, no doubt ;

" For, mother, see, my bowels gushing out."

" Don't try to keep it down !" the dame replied ;

" 'Tis not your own, dear ! but the bull's, inside ! "

So when an orphan's substance guardians spend,

And retribution comes to faithless friend,

To such, deep-groaning at disgorging hour,

Methinks this fable one might quote with power.

XXXV.

THE MONKEYS.
(P. F. 366.)

TWINS at each birth the female monkey bears,
  Yet gives not them her love in equal shares.
For, by her illstarr'd fondness one opprest
Is kill'd with kindness in her rugged breast.
The other as a useless idiot thrown
Adrift, an outcast, thrives when left alone.

Men's natures oft are such, that friendliness
In them than hate is to be chosen less.

XXXVI.

THE OAK AND THE REED.
(P. F. 179.)

A MOUNTAIN-WIND tore from its roots an oak,
A wondrous old-world plant, with sweeping stroke ;
And lodg'd it in a stream, where to and fro
The eddies sway'd it.   Close beside there grow

Upon the bank, by rippling water fed,

Unnumber'd reeds. "'Twas strange," the stout oak
said,

"That plants so frail and feeble did not fall,

"While giant oaks are riven up roots and all."

Sagely the reed made answer : "Marvel not :

"Through struggling with the blasts, a fall you got :

"If but our slender tops the light breeze fill,

"We meekly bend us with a yielding will."

So spake the reed. Our fable, look you, shows

'Tis best to bow to might, and not t' oppose.

XXXVII.

THE HEIFER AND THE BULL.
(P. F. 113.)

A HEIFER yet unbroken, roaming free,

A bull hard-work'd in ploughing chanced to see ;

And said, "Poor wretch, how grievous is thy toil !"

Nought said the bull, but still upturn'd the soil.

Soon, when the rustics held their solemn feast,

The aged bull to pasture went released ;

But ropes that bound its horns the heifer drew,

That it with blood the altar might bedew.

To whom this sentence then the elder spoke :

" 'Twas for this end they kept thee from the yoke.

" Young before old, thou dost the altar deck ;

" The axe, and not the yoke, will bruise thy neck."

XXXVIII.

THE PINE.
(P. F. 123.)

SOME woodmen, bent a forest pine to split,

Into each fissure sundry wedges fit,

To keep the void, and render work more light.

Out groan'd the pine, "Why should I vent my spite

" Against the axe, which never touch'd my root,

" So much as these curst wedges, mine own fruit ;

" Which rend me through, inserted here and there !"

A fable this, intended to declare,

That not so dreadful is a stranger's blow,

As wrongs which men receive from those they know.

XXXIX.

THE DOLPHINS AND THE CRAB.
(P. F. 116.)

'TWIXT whales and dolphins there was difference
  great:

And to them came a crab to mediate.

Just as, in states, if one of small renown

Should act peacemaker for each rival crown.

XLI.

THE LIZARD.
(P. F. 388.)

'TIS said a lizard burst its back in twain

In vain attempts a dragon's size t' attain.

Hurt to thyself will be thy certain fate,

If men far higher thou shouldst imitate.

XLII.

THE DOG AND THE COOK.
(P. F. 62.)

HIGH feast a cit was holding, at the end
Of sacrifice.   His house-dog ask'd a friend,
Whom he had met, to come and share his meal.
He came.   The cook upraised him by the heel
And toss'd him o'er the wall into the street.
Whom when each dog did with the question greet,
" What cheer ? " he said, " What more could be
        desired,
" When I scarce know by what way I retired ? "

XLIII.

THE STAG AND THE HUNTERS.
(P. F. 128.)

AN antler'd stag, athirst in midday heat,
Drank of a silent pool beneath his feet.
At these and at his hoofs he felt disdain,
As the clear stream reflected them again.

Not thus his horns with swelling heart he eyed ;
But Nemesis was near, to chasten pride.
For soon a train of huntsmen fill'd the ground,
With ample nets and keenly-scenting hound.
He saw and fled, nor stay'd to quench his thirst,
And with fleet foot across the champain burst.
A thickly-tangled wood at last he gain'd,
And found his antlers in its boughs detain'd.
" Mistaken wretch !" he cried, " with scorn to treat,
" In pride of treacherous horns, my saving feet ;
" Had those been true, these had secured retreat."

When you on your affairs deliberate,
Hold nought beforehand in a certain state.
Yet cast off nought as hopeless in disgust,
Our greatest traitors oft are hopes we trust.

XLIV.

THE BULLS AND THE LION.
(P. F. 394.)

THREE bulls together in one pasture grazed :
Of seizing these a lion's hopes were raised.
He thought their union all his aims would foil,
So with deep-festering slanders to embroil
The friends he bent his mind.   Asunder they
Became, in turns, the lion's easy prey.

If thou wouldst live securely to the end,
Distrust a foe, but hold thou fast a friend.

XLV.

THE GOATHERD AND THE GOATS.
(P. F. 12.)

TWAS snowy weather : and a goatherd led
Into a cave, he deem'd untenanted,
His goats, all-white with snow descending thick ;
But thither, as he found, had come more quick

Some hornèd wild goats, a far larger stock,

And finer, too, than his accustom'd flock.

Green shoots to them he soon began to fling :

But to his own let tedious famine cling ;

Till, when the sky grew clear, he found them dead.

Meanwhile the wild goats hurried off to tread

The trackless thickets of unpastured heights.

Hence ridicule upon the goatherd lights,

Returning goat-less.   Seeking prizes new,

He lost the profit of his old one too.

XLVI.

THE SICK STAG.
(P. F. 131.)

A STAG, whose lissome joints grew stiff, had made

A grassy couch outside a woodland shade.

Hence ample fodder to his need he found.

Till soon, to see their neighbour, gathered round

Whole tribes of beasts ; (a right good neighbour he !)

Each came, and each with his supplies made free

By thoughtless nibbling, ere it sought the wood.

Thus sank, not by disease, but want of food,

A stag that scarce had yet two crow-lives told :

Had he lack'd friends, he haply had died old !

XLVII.

THE OLD FARMER AND HIS SONS.
(P. F. 103.)

AMONG old worthies lived an ancient man

With many sons : and since his life began

To wane at last, that truth might so be taught,

He bade that there should be before him brought

A bundle of thin rods. 'Twas soon at hand.

" Now use," said he, " the strength you each command,

" To break the sticks, my sons, thus closely bound."

" Well," he rejoined, when force in vain was found,

" Then take them one by one." Each broke with ease.

" E'en thus," he cried, " my children, if ye please

" To live in union, none have power to mar

" Your bond of strength, e'en though superior far.

" But if 'twixt brothers' hearts exists a breach,

" The single rod pourtrays the fate of each."

Love between brothers is man's best of gifts,

And oft the humble to high fortune lifts.

XLIX.

THE WORKMAN AND FORTUNE.
((P. F. 316.)

CLOSE to a well a workman slept one night,

Unwittingly.　But Fortune met his sight.

He seem'd to hear ; " What ho, there, sirrah, wake !

" Lest of thy tumble I the blame should take

" Among mankind, and earn an uglier name :

" For each man's trips and haps I bear the blame,

" Howe'er his own the fault, 'tis just the same."

L.

THE FOX AND THE WOODCUTTER.
(P. F. 35.)

HARD on a fox a hunter in full chase
Was pressing.   Reynard, needing breathing-space,
Spying a woodman, cried, " By those who save,
" 'Neath yonder just-fell'd poplars let me crave
" A shelter.   To the field betray me not."
The woodman sware.   The fox a shelter got.
The hunter came, and of the man would know,
" Did the fox enter there, or onward go ?"
Said he, " I saw not ;" but his finger showed
Meanwhile to reynard's hiding-place the road.
In haste at once the hunter passing on
Believed the words.   Her hottest danger gone,
Our fox began from out the poplar-heap
With fawning tail, but spiteful grin, to peep.
The old man said, " You owe your life to me.
" 'Twas I from risk of capture set you free ;

" Be grateful therefore." " To be sure," she cried,

" For the vast help, I saw your acts supplied.

" Farewell ! The Oath-god will exact his due.

" If your voice saved me, yet your finger slew."

Let none (Heaven's purpose errs not) think to flee
The sure deserts of secret perjury.

LI.

THE WIDOW AND THE SHEEP.
(P. F. 382.)

A WIDOW kept at home a single sheep :

Out of whose fleece a larger gain to reap

She clipp'd it rudely, press'd the shears too near

Its flesh, and kept them not from wounding clear.

The smarting sheep cried : " Do not torture me,

" My blood in weight will small addition be.

" Nay, mistress, nay ! My flesh if you require,

" To kill me quick, a practis'd butcher hire.

" But if 'tis fleece and wool, not flesh, you need,

" Shearers will shear me, yet not make me bleed."

LII.

THE DRIVER AND THE WAGGON.
(P. F. 79.)

STRONG bulls to town upon their shoulders drew
A four-wheel'd wain.   Its creakings were not few.
Then was the driver wroth ; and drawing near,
He spoke so plain, it could not choose but hear.
" Thou worst of goods, will not thy groaning cease,
" Though they whose shoulders draw thee, hold their
     peace ? "

It is a base man's way, to raise a moan,
As if the toil of others were his own !

LIII.

THE WOLF AND THE FOX.
(P. F. 271.)

A HAPLESS fox fell in a wild wolf's way,
And pray'd him her old life to spare, not slay.
" I will, by Pan, I will ;" the wolf replied,
" If in thy next three words thou hast not lied."

"Well : first then," said she, " would we had not

      met !

" Next, that a *blind* wolf had my path beset !

" And, third and last," she added, " go for ever !

" I trust from this day forth to meet thee never !"

LV.

THE OX AND THE ASS.
(P. F. 104.)

WITH a she-ass, best shift his means allow'd,

A tiller yoked his only ox, and plough'd.

When these he was preparing to unyoke,

Their work being over, thus the ass bespoke

The ox : " Who carries home the old man's gear ?"

" The beast whose wont it is," said he, " 'tis clear."

E

LVI.

JUPITER AND THE MONKEY.

A BABY-SHOW with prizes Jove decreed
For all the beasts, and gave the choice due heed.
A monkey-mother came among the rest ;
A naked, snub-nosed pug upon her breast
She bore, in mother's fashion. At the sight
Assembled gods were moved to laugh outright.
Said she, " Jove knoweth where his prize will fall !
" I know, my child's the beauty of them all."

This Fable will a general law attest,
That each one deems that what's his own, is best.

LVII.

MERCURY'S WAGON AND THE ARABS.
(P. F. 141.)

HERMES had laden once a cart with lies,
And much deceit, and divers villanies.
This he essay'd to drive from race to race,
Passing near every nation's dwelling-place,
And giving each a share.   He came at last
To the Arabian land.   As this he passed,
Down brake his wagon suddenly, 'tis said,
And stuck.   The Arabs, eager for a raid,
And hoping here a merchant's precious load,
Rifled the wain, nor sent it on its road
To other tribes beyond them.   Hence I find
That false and knavish is each Arab's mind.
And, as experience proves, to Arab tongue
No particle of truth hath ever hung.

LVIII.

JOVE'S CASK.

Jove in a cask all blessings pack'd and hid,
A charge for man : but first secured the lid.
Unbridled man, agog to scan the gift
And its contents, essay'd the top to lift.
Releas'd, each blessing mounted to the sky
And would not bide below, when free to fly.
Hope only tarried.   Her the lid secured,
When closed at last.   And thus hath Hope endured
In human homes.   In her sole form we see
Earnest of all the goods, that then did flee.

LIX.

JUPITER, NEPTUNE, MINERVA, AND MOMUS.
(P. F. 155.)

Pallas, 'tis said, with Neptune and with Jove,
Which should create a thing most perfect, strove.

Jove makes the choicest of created things,

A man. A dwelling to him Pallas brings :

Neptune a bull. They gave the umpire's post

To Momus : Heaven as yet he had not lost.

And he, as was his nature, hating all,

At blaming the bull's horns to work must fall,

Because they were not set beneath his eyes,

For then he'd see to strike. Man lost the prize,

Because not open was his breast, but closed,

Else each would see his neighbour's plans exposed :

He blamed the house, because no wheels were made

Of iron at its base ; that it, convey'd

To other climes might pass with roving lord.

What purports then to us the Fable's word ?

Prefer not thou to carp : but strive to do.

Momus will nought in pleasant aspect view.

LX.

THE MOUSE THAT FELL INTO THE POT.

A MOUSE into a lid-less broth-pot fell :
Choked with the grease, and bidding life farewell,
He said : " My fill of meat and drink have I,
" And all good things : 'tis time that I should die."

Thou art that dainty mouse among mankind,
If hurtful sweets are not by thee declined.

LXI.

THE HUNTER AND THE FISHERMAN.
(P. F. 220.)

A HUNTSMAN going laden from the hill,
A fisher too, whose fish his basket fill,
As luck would have it, chanced one day to meet,
And lo ! the hunter thought the fish a treat ;

The fisherman preferr'd the hunter's game.

So they exchanged their spoil.   They did the same,

Each for a time, to suit the other's taste,

With all they took : till some one said, "You'll waste

"And mar by use the present charm of these :

"And each again will seek what used to please."

LXII.

THE MULE.
(P. F. 157.)

A MULE, in lazy manger fed on hay,

And fresh with corn, began to leap and say,

Kicking his heels, " A racer is my dam,

" And I for her a match in fleetness am."

Yet with sad visage soon his course he check'd,

Constrain'd his sire, the ass, to recollect.

LXIII.

THE HERO (OR DÆMON).
(P. F. 161.)

A GOOD man for a hero's fane assign'd
Space in his court-yard.   Here he loved to bind
Wreaths on the altars, rich libations pay,
And, sacrificing oft, devoutly pray.
" Loved hero, hail ! thy fellow-lodger bless
" With plenteous gifts."   At midnight his address
Met answer.   " Heroes can vouchsafe no good
"To man ; for these 'twere meet the Gods were sued.
" 'Tis rather all the ills that fall to men,
" That we dispense : when seeking evil then,
" Pray us !   Ask *one*, and *many* I'll bestow.
" So now to whom to sacrifice you know !"

LXIV.

THE FIR-TREE AND THE BRAMBLE.
(P. F. 125.)

A FIR-TREE and a bramble disagreed,
For the fir alway paid to self the meed
Of praise. "I'm fine, well-grown in point of size :
"And my straight top is neighbour to the skies.
"'Tis I, am roof of mansions, keel of ships :
"So much my comeliness all trees outstrips."
To whom the bramble said, "Keep well in view
"The axe, whose business is thy trunk to hew,
"And saws, that cut thee : haply thou'lt prefer
"To be the bramble, rather than the fir."

All men of mark more rank and credit gain
Than meaner folks, but still more risks sustain.

LXV.

THE CRANE AND THE PEACOCK.
(P. F. 397.)

To a bright-plumaged peacock, smart and vain,
This sharp retort fell from an ashen crane.
" Through these dull wings, whose colour you decry,
" I scream aloft, in starry heights I fly.
" You, cock-like, flap your wings. The tail you spread,
" With all its gold, is never seen o'erhead."

Rather would I in threadbare coat aspire,
Than live inglorious, tho' in rich attire.

LXVI.

THE MAN WITH TWO WALLETS.
(P. F. 359.)

PROMETHEUS was a god, an elder god :
Man, the brutes' lord, he fashion'd of the sod,
'Tis said, and round his neck two wallets hung,
Full of all ills, that rise mankind among :

One, holding others' faults, in front was thrown :
The larger, slung behind him, held his own.

Hence others' falls, methinks, men clearly see :
But when one should look homeward, blind are we.

LXVII.

THE WILD ASS AND THE LION.
(P. F. 258.)

CHASE-PARTNERS were the lion and wild ass :
That did in prowess, this in speed surpass :
A booty of fat beasts their hunt supplied,
Which into three the lion would divide.
"This first," said he, "as foremost, I shall take
"In right of kinghood.   That my equal stake
"Marks as my part.   And, for the hindmost lot,
"'Twill cause you hurt, unless you flee, I wot."

Measure your strength, nor, with a man more strong,
To company, or partnership belong.

LXVIII.

APOLLO AND JUPITER.
(P. F. 151.)

SAID the far-darter to the gods on high,
" Not one can farther shoot or throw than I."
In sport great Jove Apollo's challenge took,
And quick the lots in Mars' cap Hermes shook.
Luck was with Phœbus.   Soon the golden bow
And string he circles ; lets the arrow go,
And shoots within the gardens of the West.
Said Jove, when the same range his feet had prest,
" Space fails me, boy.   To what point can I shoot ? "
Thus without shaft he won the arrow's fruit.

LXIX.

THE HARE AND THE HOUND. .

A DOG, no novice in the chase, pursued

A rough-pawed hare, disturb'd from tangled wood,

And soon was left behind. A goatherd near,

" Fine runners beat you !" said, the hound to jeer.

Said he, " One needs must use far more despatch

" To save one's own, than other lives to snatch."

LXX.

THE MARRIAGES OF THE GODS.
(P. F. 162.)

THE Gods were wedding. Each had found a mate.

To War it chanced till last of all to wait.

And so with Insolence, left all alone,

In love he fell, and won her for his own.

So runs the Fable. Hence, devoted swain,

Where'er she goes, he follows in her train.

Oh then may Insolence, most apt to smile

On commons, and to lead them wrong the while,

Be ever from our states and nations far,

For close behind her comes her husband, War.

LXXI.

THE HUSBANDMAN AND THE SEA.
(P. F. 94.)

A COUNTRYMAN beheld a crowded ship

Its prow beneath the arching surges dip ;

"Would thou hadst ne'er been ploughed," he cried,

    "thou main !

"Harsh element, of which all men complain."

The sea o'erheard, assumed a woman's tone,

And said, "I pray you, leave my name alone.

"For 'tis not I that cause you all these woes :

"But every blast that round about me blows,

"See me and sail me, yonder winds removed,

"And gentler than your earth you'll own me proved."

Bad natures oft turn many goods to worse,

Thus e'en a blessing comes to seem a curse.

LXXII.

THE BIRDS AND THE JACKDAW.
(P. F. 200.)

A CONTEST in Heaven's courts for beauty's prize,

Bright Iris, who with the Gods' tidings hies,

Proclaim'd to birds.   The news soon spread to all,

And to himself each hoped the meed would fall.

Rose from a rock, that rarely goat had scaled,

A spring, whose clear wave ne'er in summer fail'd.

To it resorted all the feather'd race,

Intent on washing, each, its wings and face,

Shaking its wings, its plumage combing clean ;

When, lo ! a jackdaw to approach was seen,

A crow's now-ancient son.   From ev'ry plume

And each wet shoulder he made haste to assume

A stolen feather.   Soon his various guise

In the Gods' sight the eagle's form outvies.

Him Jove, astonished, victor had declared,

Had not the swallow, Pallas-like, unbared

The cheating rogue, her feathers quick to claim ;
" Pray," said the daw, "expose me not to shame."
To pluck him, next, the thrush and turtle-dove,
Tomb-haunting lark, and jay, together strove ;
The hawk, a-watch for birds not yet full grown,
Nay, all the birds.　Thus was the jackdaw known.

My son, array thee in thy proper dress :
For borrow'd clothes will leave thee garmentless.

LXXIII.

THE KITE.
(P. F. 170.)

OF old far other was the kite's shrill cry !
Till once she heard a horse neigh tunefully.
She needs must ape the steed ; and then nor heard
Her former voice, nor that which she preferred.

LXXIV.

THE MAN, THE HORSE, THE OX, AND THE DOG.
(P. F. 173.)

A HORSE, an ox, a dog, distrest by cold,

To seek the warmth of a man's house made bold.

He let them enter by his open'd door,

And was not slack to give them of his store,

Warming his guests withal beside his hearth :

The horse found corn, of vetch the ox no dearth,

While the dog shared the table of his host.

Then fain would they requite their supper's cost ;

And so its life's chief habit each bestows.

The horse gave first.   Hence each among us glows

With leaping spirit in our early prime.

The ox came next.   Therefore, at mid-life's time,

Man toils, and dearly loves to hoard and save.

The dog, 'tis said, life's latest features gave.

Whence, Branchus, each, as age steals o'er him, grows

Peevish apace, caressing only those

To whom he looks for food.   A stranger's face

Provokes his bark, and never wins his grace.

F

LXXV.

THE UNSKILFUL PHYSICIAN.
(P. F. 169.)

THERE lived a quack. And all but he could tell
A sick man not to fear; he'd soon be well :
" Diseases run their time, but then are over ;"
The doctor came and said, "You won't recover !
" Make all your preparations. You must die !
" I scorn to cheat : I'm not the man to lie.
"To morrow at the most you'll scarce get o'er ! "
He said, nor visited his patient more.
But, lo ! the man from his disorder rose,
Pallid, and somewhat shaky on his toes.
Taking his walk, the doctor met him so :
"Good morrow ! How goes on the world below ?"
"Oh ! deadly lively ! Lethe's draught is flat !
" But if you'd know what hell's high powers were at,
" Doctors just now incurr'd their fiercest threats,
" Because each sick man well so quickly gets.

" They were proscribing all.   Among the first

" They talk'd of posting you.   But forth I burst

" A little timid from the shadowy crowd,

" And suppliant before their sceptres bow'd ;

" And sware to them the truth I could not hide,

" You were no doctor, but had been belied."

LXXVI.

THE KNIGHT AND HIS CHARGER.
(P. F. 178.)

A KNIGHT his charger pamper'd day by day,

So long as war was rife, with corn and hay,

As his brave comrade in the battle's din ;

But when war ceas'd, and peace at last came in,

When from his deme the knight drew pay no more,

Oft from the woods to town his charger bore

Huge logs of timber, and with various load

Toil'd as a hireling on a weary road ;

On sorry chaff he barely life preserv'd,

And yoked for draught, no longer knighthood serv'd.

But war again was heard without the walls,

On each to burnish arms the trumpet calls,

To whet his steel, his war-horse to array :

Again our knight has bridled for the fray

His charger, led for him to take the field,

But its weak limbs began to sink and yield.

" Go rank thyself with infantry," it said :

" If thou could'st me from horse to ass degrade,

"No more can I my former self be made."

LXXVII.

THE FOX AND THE CROW.
(P. F. 204.)

A CROW upon his perch was munching cheese,

When a sly fox by arguments like these,

To suit herself, beguiled him of his prize :—

" Fair are thy plumes, good crow, and bright thine
eyes,

" Charming thy neck, an eagle's breast thou hast,

" In talons thou art by no brute surpass'd.

" 'Tis strange that dumb should be a bird so smart !"

The flatter'd crow became elate in heart,

And, cawing, from his mouth the cheese let fall ;

This reynard snatch'd, and tauntingly did call,

" 'Tis true thou wast not dumb, for thou canst speak,

" Yet, spite of all thou hast, thy mind is weak."

LXXVIII.

THE SICK CROW.
(P. F. 208.)

A sick crow to its weeping mother said,

" Weep not, but pray the Gods that from the bed

" Of sad disease and suffering I may rise."

" Will any god," said she, " child, hear my cries,

" And save thee ? Is there one of whom 'tis true,

" His altar never has been robb'd by you ?"

LXXIX.

THE DOG AND THE SHADOW.
(P. F. 233.)

TRAY from the shambles stole a piece of meat;
And, as he cross'd a stream, upon its sheet
Of crystal saw the shadow magnified;
Which, letting go the flesh, to grasp he tried.
He gain'd nor it, nor that which he had lost,
And, supperless, again the river cross'd.

All avaricious men consume in vain
Uncertain lives, in fleeting hope of gain.

LXXX.

THE CAMEL.
(P. F. 182.)

A DRINKING master would his camel bring
To dance to flutes, and brazen cymbal's ring.
" Would that I could on a plain road advance,
" Causing no laughter," said she, " much less dance."

LXXXI.

THE FOX AND THE MONKEY.
(P. F. 43.)

A FOX said to an ape, " The stone you see
" Records my sire's and grandsire's memory."
Said Pug to Reynard, " Lie, as likes you best,
" For none remain your story's truth to test."

It marks a bad man not to shrink from lies,
When, lying, he can shun detective eyes.

LXXXII.

THE LION AND THE FOX.
(P. F. 257.)

A MOUSE ran o'er a sleeping lion's mane,
And the roused brute his wrath could not restrain :
So bristling up, he leapt from out his lair.
A neighbour-fox derision did not spare,

That on a mouse the king of brutes should spend
His ire.   Said he, "I fear not, cunning friend,
" Lest mice my skin should nettle, and escape :
" But roads o'er me take an ill-habit's shape."

The boldness of the impudent repress,
Small though it be, before it can progress !
Nor let it by the mean be lightly dreamt,
That thou wilt be a butt for their contempt.

LXXXIII.

THE HORSE AND THE GROOM.
(P. F. 176.)

A GROOM each day his horse kept currying,
Yet each day too the corn-bin emptying.
Then said the horse, " If sleek you really would
" Behold me, prythee, do not sell my food."

True love will study things expedient
And useful.   Vain, indeed, is ornament
As a makeweight, when needful things are spent.

LXXXIV.

THE GNAT AND THE BULL.
(P. F. 235.)

A GNAT on a bull's horn his seat had made,
And, pausing first, thus with a buzz he said :
"If I bear down or bend your neck a whit,
"I'll go and on yon river-poplar sit."
The bull cried, "Stay or go, for aught I care,
"I did not even know when you came there."

Absurd is he, who, being nought, will try
To cope with great men, and ape something high.

LXXXV.

THE DOGS AND THE WOLVES.
(P. F. 267.)

A FEUD between the dogs and wolves arose,
And of their host the dogs as leader chose
One from Achaia : who, like general sage,
Kept holding back.   His troops began to rage

At his preferring ambush to fair fight.

" Why I delay," he answered, " hear aright,

" And why I'm careful.   Prudence can't be wrong.

" Our foes I see are one united throng ;

" But some of us have from Molossia come,

" Others from Crete, from Acarnania some :

" Some are Dolopian : others Cyprus boast,

" Or Thrace their home : in short, a various host.

" We differ, unlike these, in colour too,

" Being, some black, and some of ashen hue :

" While some are bright and mottled in the chest,

"Others are white.   Discordant bands at best

" How can I marshal, with an eye to war,

" Gainst troops that all alike in all things are ? "

For aught more good than harmony to seek
Is vain.   Disunion slavish is, and weak.

LXXXVI.

THE SWOLLEN FOX.
(P. F. 31.)

An aged oak was at its roots decay'd,

Wherein the wallet of a hind was laid,

Ragged and brimful of stale bread and meat ;

A fox ran in, and its contents did eat.

Her stomach thence, no marvel, wax'd so stout,

That through the opening she could not get out.

She wept.   Another fox, that came that way,

Said jeeringly, " Till you are fasting, stay !

" You won't find egress, till you grow as thin

" In stomach, as you were when you got in."

LXXXVII.

THE DOG AND THE HARE.
(P. F. 229.)

CHASING a mountain hare, a certain hound
Would one while bite her, if a chance he found,
And one while turn and lick her as a friend;
Said puss at last, "Let double-dealing end.
"Be a true brute.   If friend, why do you bite?
"But if a foe, why fawn, nor be downright?"

Of an uncertain class of minds are those,
Whom, if to trust or distrust, no one knows.

LXXXVIII.

THE LARK AND ITS YOUNG.

IN the green corn a lark, that nurs'd his young,
At dawn, in answer to the lapwing sung.
And now his brood had fed on corn so long,
That they had crests, and on their wings were strong.

So the field's owner, when he came to see

The harvest ripe, said, " Now 'tis time for me

" To gather all my friends, that I may reap."

But one of the young crestlings chanc'd to keep

Watch on his words, and ran, his sire to tell,

That to remove them elsewhere it were well.

But he replied, "'Tis not yet time to flee !

" Who trusts to friends, not over-fast is he."

When the man came, and saw the sun's bright ray

Had caused the ear o'er-ripe to fall away,

And said, he'd hire reapers the next morn,

And pay all hands to bind and sheave the corn,

Then the lark to his novice children cries,

" 'Tis time, my sons, that each one elsewhere flies,

" Since on himself, not friends, the man relies."

LXXXIX.

THE WOLF AND THE LAMB.
(P. F. 274.)

A WOLF beheld a lambkin once astray,

And did not give brute force at once its way,

But, bent to seize it, found this specious plea :

"Small though you were last year, you slander'd me."

"Nay ! how last year ? A year I've not been born."

"Well, then, you nibbled my own field of corn !"

"I eat nor grass nor corn ! A nursling still !"

"Have you not drunk then of my private rill ?"

"As yet, my mother's milk's my beverage."

Upsprang the wolf, and ate the lamb in rage.

"A wolf," said he, "can't for his supper wait,

"Though all his pleas you may invalidate."

XC.

THE LION AND THE FAWN.

A LION raved. A fawn from woods hard by
Saw, and began, "Ah! wretched we!" to cry.
" How must we, when he's mad, expect to fare,
" Whom, in his sane state, none of us could bear?"

XCI.

THE BULL AND THE GOAT.
(P. F. 396.)

ONCE, in a cave the goatherds had forsaken,
A bull had from a lion refuge taken,
But to contest his entrance there remain'd
One goat within, who hornèd war maintain'd.
" Pshaw!" said the bull, " could I yon beast elude,
" I'd bear a little space to see you rude!
" Just let the lion pass, and you shall note
" How wide the difference 'twixt bull and goat."

XCII.

THE TIMID HUNTER.
(P. F. 114.)

A LION-HUNTER once, who courage lack'd,
In the hill-forests dense his game had track'd.
A woodman near a tall fir met his view,
Whom by the Nymphs he pray'd, if aught he knew,
To point the wild beast's steps, that harbour'd near.
The other said, " Good luck has brought you here !
" The lion's self to you I'll quickly show."
Pale, and with chattering teeth, he cried, " No, no !"
" Pray don't oblige me, friend, beyond your task :
" To see the lion's track, not him, I ask."

XCIII.

THE WOLVES AND THE SHEEP.
(P. F. 268.)

THE wolf-tribe sent the flock an embassy,

And proffer'd oaths of peace and amity.

The terms were that the dogs should be disgraced,

Who caused the feud now sought to be effaced.

The sheep, weak, silly creatures, were disposed

To scout old friends.   An old ram interposed,

And said, his thick wool bristling from below,

" A novel mediation this, I trow !"

" How, if unguarded, am I safe with you,

" When even now my perils are not few,

" Though, while I feed, I keep my watch-dog true ?"

G

XCIV.

THE WOLF AND THE HERON.
(P. F. 276.)

A BONE in the wolf's throat was firmly set :

Then covenanted he the hern should get

A due reward, if, letting down his neck,

He'd draw the bone, and thus his suffering check.

The hern extracted it, and claim'd his prize.

" Nay," said the wolf, with grinning teeth and eyes,

" A meed of healing great enough you've found,

" Your head from out the wolf's jaw safe and sound."

It is ill wages, when the bad you aid.

To take no hurt, is to be well-repaid.

XCV.

THE SICK LION.
(P. F. 243.)

Sick in a rocky cleft a lion lay,

Glad on the ground his failing limbs to stay.

With him a fox was chiefly intimate,

To whom he said, " Wouldst have me 'scape my fate ?

" Then know, I hunger for the stag that dwells

" 'Neath yon wild pine amid the woodland dells.

" And I, you wot, can hunt the stag no more ;

" But if you choose your honied words to pour

" Into his ears and trap him, mine's the prize !"

Away went Reynard : where the wild wood lies

She found him leaping o'er the mossy grass,

And, first embracing, then began to pass

High compliments, and say she came to bring

Good news.   " My neighbour is the forest king,

" The lion ; he is sick, nay well nigh dead :

" And he was thinking who should rule instead

" O'er beasts.   To find a pig with sense is hard !

" The bear is dull ; and wrathful is the pard.

" The braggart tiger ever stands alone.

" He deems the stag is meetest for his throne.

" 'Tis light of form ; it lives unnumber'd years ;

" Fearful to reptiles is the horn it rears,

" Branching like trees, to bulls' horn un-allied ;

" Need I say more ?   The choice is ratified.

" You are to rule the beasts that roam the hills ;

" Oh ! then, whene'er the throne your highness fills,

" Pray think of Reynard, who first let you know

" These news.   I've said.   Good-bye, my dear ! I go

" To join the lion ; he may need me back :

" My counsel now in all things he would lack.

" You'll come, child, too, if the advice you heed

" Of an old head.   'Tis fitting you should speed

" To counsel him, and cheer him in his woes :

" Small things win much at life's extremest close,

" And souls are in the eyes of them that die :"

Thus spake the fox.   The stag's heart leapt on high

At her feign'd words.   He sought the cavern home

Of the wild beast, and wist not what should come.

Reckless upsprang the lion from his lair,

And fail'd, through haste, of more than just to tear

The stag's ear with his talon-tips.   Afraid,

Straight from the door it fled to woodland shade.

The fox to clap her paws in spite was fain,

Because her labour had been spent in vain.

Gnashing his teeth the lion raised a groan ;

Chagrin and famine seiz'd him, both in one.

Again he call'd the fox, again he pray'd

The stag by some fresh trick might be betray'd.

Revolving schemes from her heart's inmost core,

" I'll do your will," she said, " tho' hard, once more."

Then follow'd she, like sage dog, on the scent,

Weaving her wily tricks, as on she went ;

Asking each shepherd ever and anon,

" Knew he which way a bleeding stag had gone ?"

Each that had seen it, pointing led the way

To where, she found, the fleet stag resting lay,

Tired with the chase, in deeply shaded wood,

And there with forehead unabash'd she stood.

A shudder smote the stag in back and knees,

Wrath overflow'd his heart.   His words were these :

" Now you pursue me, wheresoe'er I fly :

" But, hated one, discomfiture is nigh,

" If you approach, and dare to mutter aught.

" Go play the fox to others yet untaught

" In wiles.   Stir others up, and make them reign."

But Reynard heard unmoved.   In blameful strain

She said, " Art thou so mean, so full of fear ?

" And dost thou thus suspect associates dear ?

" The lion planning what might profit thee,

" And how to rouse thee from past apathy,

" Just touch'd thine ear, a dying father's act,

" For he desired no precept should be lack'd

" By thee for keeping sovereignty so great ;

" But thou his weak claw's tickling couldst not wait,

" And, tearing thyself off, wast wounded sore.

" Hence he, than thou, is now offended more,

" For trial shows thee weak, unfit to trust ;

" So into kinghood he the wolf will thrust.

" Ah me ! an evil lord !   What will befall ?

" Thou art a cause of ills to one and all.

" Nay, come and show more courage than of old,

" Nor cower, like sheep just straying from the fold.

" Now may my oath by springs and leaves be known,

" So may I subject be to thee alone,

" As he intends no harm, but in good will,

" Bids thee the lordship of the beasts to fill."

Cajoling thus the brocket, him she won

Into the selfsame fate again to run.

So when he lay, inclosed within the lair,

The lion had, himself, most dainty fare,

Gorging the flesh, the marrow from each bone

And entrails lapping.   Famishing, alone

Stood the decoyer, till she slily stole

And ate the heart, which near her chanc'd to roll ;

The single gain of all her toil was this :

Which soon the lion, counting, came to miss,

Of all the inward parts.   Indignant then

He search'd each lair, and hunted every den.

And Reynard said, to cheat him of the truth,

" Don't search in vain !   It had no heart in sooth.

" To own a fine heart he was likely, who

" A second time came visitor to you !"

XCVI.

THE WOLF AND THE YOUNG RAM.

A WOLF pass'd by a wall ; and from its top
A young ram peeping much abuse let drop.
Gnashing his teeth the wolf said bitterly,
" Boast not thyself.   Thy place abuses me !"

Let no one then, whom luck or accident
Makes strong awhile, to insolence give vent.

XCVII.

THE LION AND THE BULL.
(P. F. 262.)

A LION once conceiving a design
Against a wild bull, feign'd that at the shrine
Of Cybele he meant to sacrifice,
And bade the bull ; who, blind to his device,

Promis'd to join the feast, and came and stood
At his host's door. Seeing the kitchen strew'd
With cauldrons of hot water, cleavers bright,
Sharp carving-knives, but nought for food in sight,
Save a cock bound, he to the hills made off :
Much did the lion, when he met him, scoff.
" Nay," said the bull, " this token proves I came.
" Your ample kitchens larger victims claim."

XCVIII.

THE LION WOOER.
(P. F. 249.)

A LION, smitten with a beauteous maid,
Ask'd her in marriage of her sire, who said,
Without show of dislike or hollowness,
" I'd give consent, and gladly, I profess !
" What sire a mighty lion would refuse !
" But timid are young maids' and children's views.
" Just think how large your teeth ! how long you wear
" Your talons ! What maid, do you think, will dare

" To clasp you boldly, see you unalarm'd ?

" If you would wed, against these fears be arm'd.

" Be a wild beast no more, but suitor mild."

On wings of promise, by the words beguil'd,

The lion drew his teeth, his talons pared

With surgeon's knife, then to the sire repair'd,

And showing them he claim'd his bride.   But all

With stones or clubs on him began to fall.

He lay inactive, e'en as dying swine,

Taught by a crafty old man to divine,

That 'tis not nature's will that men should burn

For lions, or they love mankind in turn.

XCIX.

THE WOLF AND THE DOG.
(P. F. 278.)

THERE met a wolf a dog exceeding sleek,

Of whom the former soon began to seek,

" In what abode he grew so fat and large."

Said he, " I live at a rich master's charge."

" But how," said Wolf, " became thy neck so bare ?"

" Rubb'd by the iron collar which I wear :

" My master had it forg'd, and placed on me."

The wolf on this made answer mockingly :

" Adieu ! for me, the nurture I refuse,

" Through which the iron is my neck to bruise."

C.

THE LION AND THE EAGLE.

(F. DE FURIA, 358.)

AN eagle to a lion flew, and pray'd

To be his partner. " What should let ?" he said

In answer. " Only you must certify,

" You will not let your faith take wings and fly :

" On friend unsettled how could I rely ?"

CI.

THE WOLF AND THE FOX.
(P. F. 272.)

A FINE-GROWN wolf his tribe in size outvied,
The rest surnamed him "lion."   Puff'd with pride
He could not bear renown, but left his kin,
And with the lions friendship strove to win.
Then said a jeering fox, " From me be far
" That frenzy, in the mists of which you are.
" For you, no doubt, to wolves a lion seem,
" But lions count you wolf, in their esteem."

CII.

THE LION RULING JUSTLY.
(P. F. 242.)

A LION ruled : no brawling lion he,
Nor fierce, nor one who used brute force with glee ;
But mild and just, as any child of man.
'Twas in his reign, or so the story ran,

The wild beasts held a congress, with this aim,

Each to do justice, and receive the same.

And when each brute accounted, as by law,

Wolves to the lambs, the pard to the chamois,

Tiger to stag, and peace pervaded all,

A cow'ring hare said, " Ever did I call

" Upon the gods, to grant this day ere long,

" Which makes the weak a terror to the strong."

CIII.

THE SICK LION AND THE WILD BEASTS.
(P. F. 246.)

A LION hunting could no longer go,

He had grown old full many a year ago.

So in his cave he laid him, feigning sick,

And gasping, not in truth, 'twas all a trick.

His once deep voice now seem'd so faint and low :

Quickly did Rumour to each beast's den go ;

Her tale, the lion's sickness, grieved them all,

And each went in, on the old king to call.

These, in their turn, he took with ease, though weak,

And, feasting on them, found his age grow sleek.

Yet one, who guess'd his trick, a fox, afar

Ask'd, " Prythee, good my liege, say how you are ?"

He answer'd, " Best of creatures, how d'ye do ?

" Come nearer, nor from far your old friend view.

" Come, sweet one, with the balm your words can

        give,

" And comfort me who have not long to live."

Said fox, " Good-bye, my leaving you'll forgive ;

" I must be off, forewarn'd by many a track

" Of beasts, which you can scarcely prove came back."

He that is taught by strange calamity

And is not first in falling, blest is he !

CIV.

THE DOG BEARING THE BELL.
(P. F. 224.)

A DOG was fond of biting "on the sly,"
Whose master, this ill trick to notify
Abroad, a brazen bell around him tied.
On this the dog began to ring with pride
His bell in every square. Then to him said
An elder dog, "Why proudly lift your head,
" Poor wretch? no badge of worth you sound in this,
" But a plain proof of what you do amiss."

CV.

THE WOLF AND THE LION.
(P. F. 279.)

A WOLF was bearing home a sheep one day
Snatch'd from the fold. A lion in the way
Captur'd his spoil. The wolf, far off, made moan:
" *Wrongly*," he cried, "you've robb'd me of my own."

The mocking lion answer'd with delight;
" Of course 'twas given by friends, and your's *by right.*"

CVI.

THE GENTLE LION.

A LION once the noblest life of men
Would emulate, and in his spacious den
" At home," with kindness to entreat essay'd
All the best kinds of beasts of hill or glade.
Large grew the crowd of various brutes apace,
For which his kindly " menage " found a space :
While each he loved and feasted as a guest,
Meting to all the food they fancied best,
He 'd ta'en a friendly fox his den to share,
With whom his life was mostly smooth and fair ;
But carver to him was an ancient ape,
Each messmate's share to parcel out and shape.
This ape, if guest unwonted cross'd the door,
Set the same meal his lord and him before,
The lion's chase some recent spoil had ta'en,

While Reynard did but scraps of stale meat gain.

So when a purposed silence she maintain'd,

And now from food and feast her paws restrain'd,

Her conduct's motive fain the host would seek:

" Sage fox, in wonted fashion, prythee, speak;

" Share, dearest, share the feast with cheerful face."

" Best," cried the fox, " of all the wild-beast race,

" With much solicitude I waste my heart;

" Nor do things present merely cause the smart;

" But what is coming, I with grief foresee:

" For if fresh guests come hither constantly,

" One after other, and this habit grows,

" I shall miss even stale meat, I suppose."

A lion's smile o'er the pleased lion came:

" I told the ape so.   Me then do not blame."

H

CVII.

THE LION AND THE MOUSE.
(P. F. 256.)

To dine on captured mouse a lion thought :
But on the verge of fate the wretch besought
(Poor household thief) the beast, in words of fear ;
" 'Twere meet that, hunting hornèd bulls and deer,
" With suchlike meat you should your paunch make
          fat ;
" But a poor mouse ! 'tis wrong such food as that
" Should ever touch your lips.   Oh, spare me, pray !
" Small as I am, this boon I may repay."
The beast let go his suppliant with a smile ;
But, himself netted in a little while,
By youthful hunters he was made secure.
Slyly the mouse stole to an aperture,
Nibbled with tiniest teeth the sturdy twine,
And let the beast again see daylight shine,
Unbound : requiting thus his former gift.

To men of sense plain is our fable's drift.

CVIII.

THE COUNTRY MOUSE AND TOWN MOUSE.
(P. F. 297.)

Two mice, of whom one spent a-field his day,
The other's hole in rich town storehouse lay,
To have their food in common both agreed :
And so the town-bred mouse came first, to feed
Where now the field was fresh with verdant fruits ;
And nibbling there the moist and bitter roots
Of corn, from dingy clods by no means free,
" The life of wretched ant is yours," said he,
" Eating scant barley in the depths of earth.
" For me—I find much plenty and no dearth.
" I dwell in plenty's horn, compared with you.
" Come and feast freely, as you'd wish to do,
" Leaving the moles to burrow in the soil."
He won the simple mouse from rustic toil,
Men's homes to enter, 'neath their walls to bore ;
And show'd him where there is of pulse a store,

A cask of figs, and where the meal-bags are ;
Where the date-chest, and where the honey-jar.
When, spurr'd and much delighted by all these,
He from a basket dragg'd a piece of cheese,
Lo ! some one oped the door ; away he leapt,
And trembling, to his hole's aperture crept,
Crowding his host, and venting hideous squeaks.
But in a while from his retreat he sneaks,
Intent a Camirœan fig to taste ;
But, after something, upon them in haste
Came some one else. They hid. The country mouse
Said, " Feast, and fare you well, in plenty's house :
" Of these abundant revels take your fill ;
" You 'll find them mainly fraught with risk and ill,
" Meanwhile, desert my smooth clod will not I,
" Where I munch barley, and all fears defy!"

CIX.

THE CRAB AND ITS MOTHER.
(P. F. 187.)

" Don't walk aslant, nor o'er the moist rock draw

" Crosswise," its dam said to the crab, " thy claw."

" Nay, first," cried he, " Mother and mentor too,

" Walk straight yourself: I'll watch and follow you."

CX.

THE DOG AND HIS MASTER.
(P. F. 227.)

" Gape not," a man about to travel cried

To his dog near him ; "but to start provide ;

" For you must go with me."   It wagg'd its tail,

And said, " I'm right ! 'Tis you in quickness fail."

CXI.

THE ASS CARRYING SALT.
(P. F. 322.)

A HUCKSTER, who contrived an ass to keep,
Hearing that salt on the sea-coast was cheap,
Chose to invest in it.   With goodly load
Homeward he drove.   When fairly on the road,
Into a stream the ass unconscious rolled,
And, the salt melting, had no weight t' uphold,
So rose with greater ease, and lightly sought
And reach'd the bank.   More salt the owner bought;
Again he brought his ass to load : again
Piled his bags heavier.   Then, in toil and pain,
Crossing the stream that caused his former fall,
The ass, on purpose, slipt, lost salt and all;
And, at his luck triumphant, lightly rose.
Now did the huckster a new scheme propose;
'Twas this :—" To carry inland from the sea
" Whole loads of porous sponges : salt-bags he

"Was sick of." So the ass, in knavish sort,

When to the stream again his load he brought,

Fell down on purpose. Every sponge was soak'd

At once, and he to heavier burden yoked ;

Home on his back he bore a double bale.

Where men have oft succeeded, they may fail.

CXII.

THE MOUSE AND THE BULL.

A BULL was bitten by a mouse. In pain

He tried to catch it : but 'twas first to gain

The mouse-hole. With his horns, to raze its walls,

The bull essays, until asleep he falls,

Sinking, fatigued, hard by. Forth straightway hies

The peeping mouse, bites him again, and flies.

Uprose the bull, perplext what now to do,

And the mouse squeak'd to him this moral true :

"Not always mighty are the great. 'Tis seen

"Sometimes, that stronger are the small and mean."

CXIII.

THE SHEPHERD AND THE DOG.
(P. F. 371.)

A MAN about to fold his sheep at eve,

Was going a yellow wolf with them to leave

Penn'd up.   The sheep-dog saw, and said, "What haste

     haste

" To save the sheep, you bring *him* in to waste?"

CXIV.

THE LAMP.
(P. F. 285.)

A LAMP that swam with oil, began to boast

At eve, that it outshone the starry host,

And gave most light to all.   Her boast was heard:

Soon the wind whistled: soon the breezes stirred,

And quench'd its light.   A man rekindled it,

And said, "Brief is the faint lamp's boasting-fit,

" But the star-light ne'er needs to be re-lit."

CXV.

THE TORTOISE AND THE EAGLE.
(P. F. 419.)

ONCE to the divers, gulls, and wild sea-mews
A sluggish tortoise thus expressed her views.
" Would that I, too, had had the luck to fly!"
An eagle chanced to hear, and made reply :
" Tortoise, how much shall be the eagle's prize,
" If to the air he makes thee lightly rise ?"
" Thou shalt have all and each of ocean's gifts !"
" Agreed !" the eagle cries, and lightly lifts
The other to the clouds, upon her back,
Then lets her fall, and on the hill-side crack
Her brittle coat of shell. He heard her cry,
At the last gasp : " I well deserve to die !
" Where was to me of clouds and wings the need,
" Who on my mother earth could make no speed?"

CXVI.

THE HUSBAND AND THE GALLANT.

A youth was singing sweetly at mid-night :
A wife that heard him, rose, and in delight
Peep'd from her windows, whence a view she had,
By the bright moon-beam, of a handsome lad.
She therefore left her spouse asleep to snore,
Came down the halls, and passed without the door,
And quickly gain'd the object she desired.
Her husband rose in haste : his eyes enquir'd
Where was his mate, whom in the home he lack'd ?
Soon did the song his doubting steps attract.
Then cried he to his wife, " Be not dismay'd,
" This youth within our house to sleep persuade."
He took him in : the youth found both were bent
To please, and of the wife grew negligent.
So runs the fable.   Read its moral right,
'Tis ill to triumph, when one may requite.

CXVII.

THE MAN AND MERCURY.
(P. F. 118.)

THE sea engulfed a ship and all its crew,
Which one beholding this conclusion drew,
" That the gods rule unjustly : for that they
" A host of harmless men agreed to slay,
" Because one godless wretch was in the ship."
But as the words were just upon his lip,
A swarm of ants surprised him, urged by haste
('Tis nothing strange), some barley chaff to taste.
Stung by one ant, on all the grumbler trod :
Hermes appear'd, and tapp'd him with his rod.
Said he, " Will you not let the Gods then do
" To you that justice, the ants meet from you ?"

CXVIII.

THE SWALLOW THAT DWELT NEAR THE JUDGES.

(P. F. 418.)

ACCUSTOM'D ever to men's haunts to cling,
Her nest a tawny swallow built in spring
On walls, that skirted some old judges' homes;
Where of seven nestlings mother she becomes;
Nestlings, unfringed with purplish feathers yet;
And these, each one in turn, a serpent ate,
Gliding from out his hole.   The bird forlorn
Forthwith began, in words like these, to mourn
For her ill-fated babes, untimely ta'en:
" Alas, my sad fate," thus did she complain,
" Since, where men's laws and ordinances are,
" Thence a poor swallow, injured, flies afar."

CXIX.

THE IMAGE OF MERCURY.

A MAN, a craftsman, cherish'd, wrought in wood,
A Hermes, before whom each day he stood
With offerings of meat and drink : yet still,
Much to his indignation, he fared ill.
He took the image by its leg, and dash'd
It on the ground ; so when its head was smash'd,
Out fell some gold.   He pick'd it up, and said,
" Ungrateful God to friends, and wrong of head !
" For when we served thee, thou didst nowise aid,
" But when we scoff'd, our wrongs with good hast
        paid.
" Would I had known before that nought was due,
" Save this new service, Mercury, to you."

In fables Æsop gods doth introduce,
To teach us how to act in daily use.
Honour to cross-grain'd folks is toil in vain ;
Insult them, and their kindnesses you gain.

CXX.

THE FROG PHYSICIAN.
(P. F. 78.)

THAT tenant of the swamp, and friend of shade,
The frog, who in the dykes his dwelling made,
Came on dry land, and thus each creature told :
" I am a doctor, who the science hold
" Of drugs more rare than Pœan's art can reach,
" Whom high Olympus deems the heavenly leech."
" How then," asked Reynard, " if you others cure,
" Your own sad lameness come you to endure ? "

CXXI.

THE HEN AND THE CAT.
(P. F. 16.)

A HEN was sick. To her a cat inclined
Her head. " How do ? For what have you a mind ?
" I'll get you all you wish. But don't say ' die !'"
" If you'll be off," said she, " that will not I."

CXXII.

THE ASS AND THE WOLF.
(P. F. 334.)

An ass went lame, from treading on a stake;

He spied a wolf, and fearing he might take

Death for his certain doom, said, "Wolf, I die :

" Hear my last breath : I'd rather thou wert nigh

" To sup on me, than vulture, or than crow.

" Yet this slight harmless boon on me bestow;

" The splinter from my foot extract, I pray;

" That painless thus my soul may wing its way

" To Hades." "This I grudge not," he replied.

T' extract the stake his teeth their aid supplied.

But now the ass, his pain and anguish sped,

Kick'd the gray gaping wolf, and turn'd, and fled,

When he had bump'd his snout, and grinders too.

" Ah !" said the wolf, "this luck to me is due !

" Why was it that to cure the lame I took,

" Who from the first knew nought, but how to cook?"

CXXIII.

THE HEN THAT LAID GOLDEN EGGS.
(P. F. 343.)

WHEN golden eggs a fine hen daily laid,
Its owner thought to find his fortune made
From endless treasure in its bowels stored :
He slaughter'd it, to pounce upon the hoard.
Its inward parts like other birds he found,
And mourn'd his baffled hopes with grief profound.

Thus oftentimes doth greediness of more
Rob men of even what they had before.

CXXIV.

[Compare Part II. Fable LII.]

THE TRAVELLER AND TRUTH.
(P. F. 314.)

In a lone spot, with no one by her side,

And much cast down, a traveller espied

A noble dame, who seem'd in evil case.

Said he, " Why dost thou tarry in this place ?

' What ails thee, lady ?   Who art thou, in sooth ?"

" If thou wouldst know," she answer'd, " I am Truth !"

At this amazed, the traveller ask'd her, " Why,

" Haunting lone spots, from cities dost thou fly ?"

To which the goddess of deep mind replied,

" Because aforetime there were few that lied.

" But now hath falsehood spread o'er all mankind,

" And if thou'lt hear, and I may speak my mind,

" Man's life in these days evil we shall find."

CXXV.

THE ASS AND THE LAP-DOG.

[Compare Part II.   Fable LIV.]

(P. F. 331.   F. DE FURIA, 367, P. 150.)

A MAN a Maltese dog kept, and an ass;
The latter, as was usual, corn and grass
Ate in a courtyard, to a manger tied ;
But graceful gambols were the pet-dog's pride,
While round its lord with various leaps it pressed,
And oft by him was fondled in his breast,
A pleasant toy, of solaces the best.
The ass meanwhile was used to grind by night
The grain of Ceres, fetching, while 'twas light,
Wood from the hill, things needful from the field ;
Hence did his spirit to sore anguish yield
To see the whelp in luxury's own lap.
Losing no time his manger's bonds to snap,
With awkward capers to the hall he came,
With what strange fawning ! What attempts at game !

The table thrown into the midst he smash'd,

And all the plates at once to atoms dash'd.

Next, near his master as he supp'd, he drew,

His hoofs, to hug him, o'er his back he threw :

But now the servants marking how he fared

From this rough usage that the ass had dared,

To save their master, interposing, rushed

And rescued him, when he was well-nigh crush'd.

Then, as the ass was gasping his last breath,

(With cornel clubs they beat him near to death,)

Said he, " As I deserv'd, a luckless ass,

" I suffer !   Wherefore did I scorn to pass

" My days among the mules ?   Why, wretchedly,

" A tiny lap-dog's rival strive to be ? "

All are not fit for every fate, be sure :

Nor is the lot of envious men secure !

CXXVI.

THE PLAYFUL ASS.
(F. DE FURIA, 368, P. 151.)

MOUNTING a roof, an ass the tiling broke
With his rough sport; whom with a switch's stroke
A man compell'd his downward course to track.
The ass to him who outraged thus his back
Remark'd, " Why, yesterday, and ere that too,
" An ape by this same sport delighted you."

CXXVII.

THE FOWLER, PARTRIDGE, AND COCK.
(F. DE FURIA, 369.)

UPON a bird-catcher a friend dropt in,
His meal of herbs just going to begin.
Nought had the bird-cage. Nothing had he caught.
So he to slay a speckled partridge thought,

A bird he'd tamed and kept for a decoy ;

But thus it pray'd that he would not destroy

Its life : " How will you manage with your net

" In fowling henceforth ?   Who for you will get

" Together a bright flock of social birds ?

" To the sweet music of what minstrel's words

" Will you repose ? "   He set the partridge free,

And chose a bearded cock for butchery.

But from its perch a crowing voice was borne,

" Whence will you learn, how much it wants to morn,

" When you have slain the hour-seer ? or know,

" When sleeps Orion of the golden bow ?

" Who shall of morning duties monish you,

" What time the bird-trap now is moist with dew ? "

" True ! you," quoth he, " the useful hours divine,

" Yet must my friend have wherewithal to dine ! "

CXXVIII.

[Compare Part II.   Fable LI.]

JUPITER THE JUDGE.
(P. F. 152.)

JOVE order'd Hermes to write each man's sin
On earthen tablets, and to pile them in
A coffer : thus to make bad men atone.
But as the tablets in a heap were thrown,
Into Jove's hands, at every settling day,
Some quickly, others slowly find their way.
We must not therefore be surprised, if some
Early do ill, but late to judgment come.

CXXIX.

THE ANT AND THE GRASSHOPPER.
(P. F. 401.)

In winter time, an ant dragged forth, to dry,

Some corn, by him last summer heap'd on high.

A starved grasshopper begg'd that he would give

Some share to it, lest it should cease to live.

"What did you," asked he, "all the summer long?"

"I lagg'd not, but was constant in my song."

Laughing, the ant said, as he barr'd his wheat,

"Dance in the cold, since you sang in the heat!"

Of needful things 'tis better thought to take,

Than joy and revels our mind's study make.

FRAGMENT I.

THE SHEEP AND THE SHEPHERD.
(LACHMANN, 130.   P. F. 317.)

[Compare Part II. Fab. LIII.]

A SHEEP one day addressed its shepherd thus :
" You keep our fleeces after shearing us ;
" Our teeming milk you drain, and turn to cheese.
" Your countless lambs, *our* young, not *yours*, are
        these ;
" We get no gain, I wot !   But all the earth,
" E'en on the hills, for thee gives verdure birth,
" Gives tender herbage, laden with the dew ;
" These are our food, yet at no cost to you.
" Yon dog the while midst us, to you so cheap,
" On as good food as feeds yourself, you keep.
The dog o'erheard and said, " Were I elsewhere
" And not amongst you, yours were sorry fare.
" Now, running round about you every way,
" The inroads of the wolf and thief I stay."

END OF PART I.

THE

FABLES OF BABRIUS.

PART II.

FABLE I.

PROEM.

SON, to this second book thine ear incline.

Should it embitter thee far more than brine,

Yet afterward a sweeter taste I leave

Than honey. Yet not me, I pray, receive

As him that spake these fables. They belong

To Sardian Æsop, whom most grievous wrong,

And god-abhorr'd, at Delphian hands befell.

So *ill* they treated one who sang so *well*.

Fools that they were, they forced him down a steep,

And left their sons a hateful name to keep.

THE LARK BURYING ITS FATHER.

(P. F. 211. ARISTOPH. AV. 471, &c.)

AMONG old saws this also Æsop said :
'Ere other birds, 'ere e'en the earth was made,
A first existence had the tufted lark ;
Whose darling child reach'd life's allotted mark,
And death, it chanced, by some disorder met.
Now, as the earth was not in being yet,
She knew not where, (how should she?) to inter
Her dead.   Five days 'twas left expos'd by her :
Then, sore perplex't, for grave she lent her head.

'Tis holy, gather hence, t' entomb the dead :
And filial love is a time-honour'd thing,
Of laws the best ; and nature's ordering.

III.

ÆSOP IN A DOCKYARD.
(P. F. 19.)

AT leisure to indulge in seeing sights,

The gaze of Æsop on a dockyard lights.

He chanced on shipwrights there, with nought to do,

Who at the sage their gibes full rudely threw,

And by their mocking challenged his reply.

His words in this not pointless fable lie.

" Chaos and Water from the first had been ;

" But Jove desired that Earth, till then unseen,

" Above the mass of waters should arise :

" Then did he her 'to swallow thrice' advise

" ' The waterfloods.'   At the first draught she made,

" Behold the mountains in their height display'd.

" When now the earth her second gulp had ta'en,

" Naked to view stood many a grassy plain.

" And should she soon to take a third see fit

" Your craft, methinks, will straight her craftsmen quit."

Who use to betters silly words and light,
Alway against themselves the laugh invite.

IV.

THE EAGLE AND THE MAN.
(P. F. 6.)

AN eagle once was netted by a hind ;
Who, having clipp'd its wings, no more confined
Its freedom midst the birds about his cot.
A fowler soon this bird by purchase got,
Let its wings grow, that late had been cut short,
And kept it thus for purposes of sport.
Soon it essay'd a flight, and seized a hare,
A gift 'twas glad to its new lord to bear.
A fox looked on, and to the eagle said :
" To thy first lord, not this, be honour paid,
" Lest he again should catch thee in his toil,
" And thee, by clipping, of thy wings despoil."

These words the sacred eagle's answer are :
" Good men I must respect, from bad keep far."

V.

THE GOAT AND THE VINE.
(P. F. 404.)

A vine with foliage and ripe clusters bloom'd.

Its shoots a goat with nibbling tooth consumed,

Whom thus the vine addrest : "Why injure me?

"And browse my leaves? Is there no grass for thee?

"Yet thou ere long thy just deserts shalt meet.

"Though now my shoots thou to the quick dost eat,

"To me no less shall satisfaction rise,

"When juice o'er thee I pour in sacrifice."

VI.

THE LION AND THE MAN.
(P. F. 63.)

A lion and a man, together thrown,

Held conversation each in boastful tone.

Their gaze, in walking, on a statue lit,

A man astride a lion, strangling it.

The man this sculpture bade the lion see,
And said, "O'er lions note our mastery."
" Nay," said the beast, "if lions only knew
" The sculptor's art, on mortals not a few ·
" By lions crush'd and strangled you might gaze."

Each doth himself in his own talk be-praise.

VII.

THE SWAN AND THE GOOSE.
(P. F. 215.)

To feed a swan, one purchase with a goose,
A different reason did a man induce.
One for the table, one for song was fed.
So when he came the goose's blood to shed,
(It had been fatted for its master's board,)
Night, drawing on, her film o'er all things pour'd.
Best of all times for catching birds is night;
Yet fail'd the owner to distinguish right
Which was the swan, and which the goose might be—
Hence for the goose, by accident left free,

Away to doom the tuneful swan was led ;

But when his song his species heralded,

That song was able to postpone his end.

Speech used in season many doth befriend.

VIII.

THE FROGS.
(P. F. 74.)

In marshy swamp two frogs were wont to bide.

When in the summer season this was dried,

They left it, for another home to look,

And in their road a well of water took.

Beholding this, thus spake the first of these :

" Into this well descend we, if you please,

" Since both for food and dwelling it bids fair."

The other said, with blame-suggestive air,

" Nay, but suppose this too should chance to fail,

" How from a depth so great could we avail

" To re-ascend ? "

Hence learn a moral true,

Without forethought 'tis useless aught to do.

IX.

THE FROGS ASKING A KING.
(P. F. 76.)

THE curse of anarchy the frogs annoy'd ;

Who to Heaven's throne an embassy employ'd,

To ask, if Jove would furnish them a king.

He knew the frog was but a silly thing ;

So order'd Hermes right into the bog

To throw, for king of croakers, a mute log.

As the log fell, the waters felt the blow,

And the frogs hasten'd to the depths below,

In terror for the moment at the sound.

But a short space, after these things, went round ;

And when they saw their sov'reign motionless,
They cast off fear, scorn only to profess;
So much so, that on it they boldly stept,
And mounted there, seats undisputed kept.
Such king to own, occasion'd high disdain;
And up they went to the Gods' courts again,
Where they the chief of rulers much besought
To send them such a monarch as they ought
To have. "That beam was quite unfit to sway
"Mute logs, far more such living beings as they.
"That stump was grown but to be food for fire."
Next Jove sent down an eel for their desire.
They saw that this was also a mere fool,
And would not have it over them to rule.
A third legation then they sent to Jove,
With earnest pray'r their second king to move,
And give them one with better sense supplied,
Fitly o'er them with justice to preside.
Their message, heard, led Jove offence to take,
And send them for their king a water-snake;
Who, getting all in turn within his power,
Did each poor frog with ruthless maw devour;

No more to cry "coäx," no more to croak !

Such fate too many of mankind provoke,
When from old rulers they their love revoke.

X.

THE ARCHER AND THE EAGLE.
(P. F. 4.)

An archer at an eagle took his aim.
The shaft he sent, true to the eagle came.
To whom when, as he turn'd his head, 'twas known,
The shaft was wing'd with feathers of his own ;
" Ah ! luckless me !" his dying accents said ;
" With mine own feathers I have made my bed."

Most from their own, much loss have sufferèd.

XI.

THE OXEN AND THE WAGON.

[Compare Part I. Fable LIL. P. F. 79.]

THEIR wain some oxen to a village drew,
And at its creaking axle wrathful grew.
Turning to it, they said, "Why creak you thus?
" When all the burden has been laid on us."

When others work, some call the toil their own,
And, over what they had no hand in, moan.

XII.

THE FROGS.
(P. F. 75.)

Two frogs were dwelling each to other near;
Now one abode in a deep marshy mere,
Which at no distance from the highroad lay;
One in a puddle on the carriage-way.

He of the mere the other recommends

To change his quarters, come, and live as friends,

And thus a safer dwelling to obtain.

The other said, declining, "'Twould be pain

" Too great for him accustom'd haunts to quit,"

And held his way, till passing over it

A wagon came ; by which the frog was crushed,

And thus on fate, by not complying, rush'd.

XIII.

THE VAGRANT PRIESTS OF CYBELE.
(P. F. 290.)

For common use to Rhea's vagrant priests

Was sold an ass, most luckless among beasts,

That it might carry for these begging knaves

Rites, food, whate'er from thirst or hunger saves.

These roam'd, as is their wont, the country through,

And craved provisions, asking, " Who but knew,

" Among the swains, how Attis fair was maim'd ?

" To Rhea's drum who would not be ashamed

" To fail in gifts of first-rate pulse and bread ? "

At length the ass, o'erburden'd, fell down dead,

Poor wretch, and said good-bye to all his toil.

Him the rogues hasten'd of his hide to spoil,

And stretch'd it, closely-fitted, o'er a drum :

On other roguish priests they chanced to come,

As they were roaming through the villages,

Furnished with drums.   And they were asked by
        these,

How fared their ass.   "It died long time ago,"

They answered, " yet it now receives a blow

" So often, that, had it been still alive,

" 'Neath these it could by no means long survive."

XIV.

THE HUSBANDMAN AND THE EAGLE.
(P. F. 92.)

A RUSTIC saw an eagle in the snare,

And, as he much admired its beauty rare,

He loosed it from its fetters forth to roam :

Thence did the eagle a warm friend become

To its preserver.   For, t' avoid the heat

And catch the breeze, it saw him take his seat

Beneath a wall.   It snatch'd, as o'er it flew,

A burden from his head, and this it threw

Far off.   The rustic, eager to pursue

His pack, made for it.   Down the walling fell :

And thus the rustic was requited well.

Kind acts, if birds in grateful memory set,

Can any, save the worst of men, forget ?

XV.

THE HUSBANDMAN AND FORTUNE.
(P. F. 101.)

GOLD, as the earth he dug, a labourer found,
And every day with garlands wreath'd the ground,
Seeing that thence he reap'd undoubted good;
But with this speech dame Fortune o'er him stood :
" Why ever, man, dost thou my gifts mistake
" For earth's ?   'Twas I that did thy riches make,
" I, by whose help 'tis said that some are blest,
" Who chance to find me kinder than the rest;
" And those unblest, to whom bad luck I bring.
" Now I enrich thee thus, as purposing
" To try thy judgment, while this wealth I send,
" Whether thou wilt it well or ill expend.
" 'Twere meet, thou shouldst feel gratitude to me ;
" For if thy nature changed with times should be,
" And thou unworthily shouldst squander all,
" On me, and not on earth, the blame would fall."

If any to thee do an office kind,
See that they never thee unmindful find.

XVI.

THE WOMAN AND HER MAIDSERVANTS.
(P. F. 110.)

A VERY careful dame, of busy way,
Kept maids at home, and these, ere break of day,
She used to rouse as early as cock-crow.
They thought 'twas hard to be awaken'd so,
And o'er wool-spinning be at work so long;
Hence grew within them all a purpose strong
To kill the house-cock, whom they thought to blame
For all their wrongs.   But no advantage came.
Worse treatment than the former them befell;
For when the hour their mistress could not tell
At which by night the cock was wont to crow,
She roused them earlier, to their work to go.
A harder lot the wretched maids endured.

Bad judgment oft hath such results procured.

XVII.

THE WIZARD WOMAN.
(P. F. 112.)

A WOMAN boasted the divining art,

And that, when Gods make the wrongdoer smart,

Her spells could bar the curse of ancient sin.

Large fee paid those who would her secret win.

She found this trade all arts of life surpass'd ;

So when the witch much substance had amass'd,

Some, on this charge, an accusation wrote,

And she was sentenced by a fateful vote.

One saw her led away for death, and cried :

" What ! was it not thy promise and thy pride,

" From other mortals wrath divine to turn ?

" Thy jurors' votes why didst thou fail to earn

" By thy persuasion ? This escaped thy plan,

(" Thinking t' upset things sacred, and to man

" The counsels of the Gods-above unseal,

" And how much anger they toward sinners feel,)

" To avert thy dragging o'er the fatal way."

A just atonement lying prophets pay.

XVIII.

AFFLICTED with disorder in the eyes,

An ancient dame a famous doctor tries,

In hopes that he her malady may cure.

Now 'twas agreed, before a witness sure,

That if that woman's eyesight he should save,

An ample fee the oculist should have :

But if the healer rid not of disease

His patient, he should forfeit all his fees.

As then with oils he did her eyes anoint,

And of his daily visit made a point,

Blindfolding her withal, her sight to shade,

Free with his patient's property he made.

Thus he continued every day to do,

And when he by degrees her goods withdrew,

And all her stock had actually ta'en,

At last the woman did her sight regain.

Of course the healer further claim'd his fee.

The dame, with sight recover'd, fail'd to see

Aught of her chattels, and refused to pay

A doctor, who with these had made away.

The healer pressed his suit, his payment sought;

She put him off, and would not pay him aught.

Before the courts he therefore brings the case,

And then the woman, standing face to face

Before the jurors, told them all the truth :

" This doctor, gentlemen, pretends, in sooth, ·

" He heal'd mine eyes, which healing balms did need;

" But I maintain that blindness sore indeed

" I suffer still ; for with mine ailing eyes

" I saw goods, chattels, riches, all I prize,

" At home.   But now, when yon rogue says I see,

" Not one of these, I say, is seen by me."

'Tis thus, to love of gain when bad men yield,

By their own hands their doings are reveal'd.

XIX.

THE DOGS AND THE FOX.
(P. F. 219.)

ONE day some dogs a lion's skin had found ;
To tear it hasten'd each audacious hound ;
And when a fox their impudence beheld,
" If still," said she, "his place the lion held
"Amid the living, ye should find his claws
"Would, oh! how much, surpass your feebler jaws."

To lesser men who, left alone, assail
An absent better, use this simple tale !

XX.

THE DRAGON AND THE EAGLE.
(P. F. 120.)

A DRAGON and an eagle fiercely met,

Contending, which should which as captive get.

The dragon got the eagle 'neath his yoke,

And bound him fast, so as almost to choke.

A farmer saw, and loosed the dragon-chain,

And bade the eagle roam at large again.

At this the dragon deep resentment bore,

And in the farmer's cup did venom pour.

So when he was about to lift it up,

Not knowing its contents, and drain the cup,

On this the eagle pounced with flapping wings,

And from the farmer's grasp the vessel flings.

Thus him that saved him did the eagle save,

Thus to his champion grateful succour gave.

XXI.

THE BEES AND THE SHEPHERD.
(P. F. 288.)

SOME busy bees, beneath an old oak's roots
Were making wax of gather'd flowers and fruits.
A shepherd saw them in sweet toil partake,
And of their comb a capture fain would make.
Round him they buzz'd, outvying one another
T' avert the theft, the thief with stings to smother.
At last the shepherd, stung and smitten sore,
Exclaim'd, "I go! no honey want I more,
" If I must needs encounter stings of bees!"

Keep from another's goods, and dwell at ease.

XXII.

THE SHIPWRECK'D MAN AND THE SEA.
(P. F. 94.)

A SHIPWRECK'D man, by ocean cast ashore,

Slept when his weary toil at last was o'er ;

But, in a while, up-rising out of sleep,

He blamed with many a charge the treach'rous deep :

Saying, that she had sailors oft beguiled,

Wearing for these a surface calm and mild,

And a fair face, betokening placid seas,

And yet o'erwhelm'd them, if they tried the breeze.

But she to him in words like these replied :

" Sailor, who crossest oft the ocean-tide,

" The winds, not me, I pray thee, learn to blame :

" For my calm nature ever is the same,

" As thou beholdest even at this hour ;

" But when, unlook'd for, boist'rous tempests lour,

" With anger'd waves my depths they agitate."

Let blame on causes, not their agents, wait.

XXIII.

THE FOX AND THE MONKEY.
(P. F. 44.)

A DEEP-TONED ass, with over-weening bray,

Proclaim'd to every beast a congress-day.

The meeting's object was a king to name,

From whose wise rule the brutes might justice claim.

An ape amongst them danced to music's sound,

And hence as king of beasts was named, and crowned.

The envious fox was bent to play the cheat:

Fixt in some nets she saw a piece of meat,

And led the monkey to the guilesome snare,

Saying, "I've found a treasure vast and rare,

"A prize, by human custom, due to kings."

Into the nets the monkey thus she brings.

Said Reynard, mocking, " Being such a fool,

" Dost think, good ape, among the beasts to rule ?

Fare as befits thee, and not ill thou'lt fare ;

But over-strength will heavier damage share.

XXIV.

JUPITER, PROMETHEUS, PALLAS, AND MOMUS.
[Compare Part I. LIX. P. F. 155.]

PROMETHEUS, Jove, and the Tritonian maid,

That each would make one thing, agreed and said.

Jove made a bull; Prometheus fashion'd men;

Pallas a dwelling. Envious Momus then

Was critic. He, of hatred ever full

To works divine, said, " Jove had spoil'd the bull;

" Whereas o'er horns he should have placed the eyes,

" Eye below horn in Jove's construction lies."

Prometheus was to blame : he fail'd to place

Man's mind outside, " that none in actions base

" Might lack detection, each might plainly read

" Of what each sev'ral man stood most in need."

Nor did the work of Pallas pass unblamed;

" Unfixt, of right, should be the house she framed,

" With wheels beneath, that if an evil one

" Should sojourn near, with ease it might begone."

Justly was Jove with Momus wroth, I wot,
Who the gods' gifts to censure scrupled not.

My son, this fable's teaching is not small ;
Into oblivion do not let it fall.
For ever toward mankind the gods are good ;
Yet, not e'en these escape maligners rude ;
And if, in fact, gods could not Momus flee,
What must not men endure from such as he ?

XXV.

THE TRUMPETER.
(P. F. 386.)

A HERALD to the fight the host did stir :
No warrior he, but a good trumpeter.
Now he, when taken, to his captors spake,
" My life, for I am guiltless, do not take ;
" For never man in the wild battle-plain
" Have I, nor e'en my faithful trumpet, slain.
" No metal beside this do I possess."
This was to him their answer pitiless :

" Why, 'tis for this thou art about to die,

" More than all else.   Thou giv'st the battle-cry

" To others, though no fighter."

That man kills,

Who any work, through which we die, fulfils.

XXVI.

HERCULES AND PALLAS.
(P. F. 159.)

Along a narrow lane went Hercules ;

And something sheep-like on the ground he sees,

Which with his club t' exterminate he tries ;

But it, once struck, began to grow in size.

Seeing it to such bulk so quickly swell,

To heavier blows with all his might he fell.

To wondrous bulk again the monster rose,

And block'd the way, all passage to oppose.

Hercules marvell'd how the thing would end,

Cast down his club, and halted.   Where to wend

He knew not.   Lo ! Athena met his sight.

" Spare toil," quoth she, " and, hero, learn aright,

" *Strife* is the strange appearance which you see.

" Let it but, as before, unhinder'd be,

" And unincreas'd 'twill bide.   In contest thus

" Swoll'n, as you see, it masters all of us."

XXVII.

HERCULES AND PLUTUS.

(P. F. 160.)

BIDDEN to feast at each immortal's side,

The hero once with men, now deified,

Sweet converse with each God held Hercules,

Till he had come to Plutus, last of these.

To speak to him the hero's soul disdain'd,

Nor converse with him, like the rest, maintain'd.

Jove in amazement for an answer press'd,

Why he had ev'ry other God address'd,

But not one syllable to Plutus said.

Then Hercules to Jove this answer made :

" Why, because him, abhorr'd on earth by me,

" I never saw but in rogues' company."

XXVIII.

THE APPLE-TREE, POMEGRANATE, AND BRAMBLE.

(P. F. 38$.)

FOR beauty's prize once strove the apple-tree

With the pomegranate.   Each strove angrily.

The thorn-inflicting bramble, dwelling nigh,

Heard all the strife, and utter'd language high

To both.   " Let us from rivalry desist

·" For beauty's prize, my friends."

                              Bid that man list

This fable, who himself, tho' vastly less,

Would thrust mid nobler men, through foolishness.

XXIX.

THE TRAVELLERS AND THE CROW.
(P. F. 312.)

As men to work did from a village go,
Upon their path came suddenly a crow,
Flying above, and blind in his left eye :
And one man said that this was reason why
They should turn back : the omen did not bode
Good luck to them, if they pursued their road.
Not without wit the other answer'd thus :
" How could that bird tell aught of fate to us,
" Which not her own bereavement had foreknown,
" Or round her eyes a guard she would have thrown."

.

XXX.

THE KITE AND THE SNAKE.
(P. F. 207.)

BEARING aloft a snake the kite up-flew,

Whom with a bite its captive turning slew,

And thus addrest him, as he breath'd his last :

" Into such phrensy wherefore wast thou cast,

" As to have injured me, who hurt thee not ?

" What thou for me designedst, is thy lot."

XXXI.

LIES AND TRUTH.

A HAUGHTY troop unto a village hies,

A muster strong of over-ruling Lies.

Of broider'd purple were the robes they wore ;

Each of their steeds its golden cheek-piece bore.

Behind, a throng audacious follow'd quick,

Deceit and Guile, and every knavish Trick.

And lo! they met a maiden on their road,

Her dress and fashion of a simple mode,

Nay, somewhat poor.　Yet stately was her mien,

And long unfed, poor sufferer, had she been.

Her did these Lies accost, and sought to know

Whither, and on what errand she would go.

She answer'd, " Pardon, sirs, if no reply

" Comes from a throat with thirst and hunger dry."

So then the Lies thus answer'd her again :—

" To yon near village follow in our train ;

" 'Tis but a small one, yet 'tis well supplied :

" Well-victuall'd hostels will good cheer provide ;

" Come as our guest, and you shall eat your fill."

She followed them, deject, and downcast still,

Into the inn : but ne'er a word she said.

Mine host on their arrival quickly spread

For them a table fill'd with various meats,

Whence each one, as he lists, his fancy treats.

This done, they bridled steeds, and cried to " horse !"

When for his reckoning asks the host, of course.

On this the Lies were wroth at his demand,

Which they nor paid, nor yet would understand.

The brood of impudence in vain he sues :

They answer straight, "That he has had his dues,

" That they have paid, like gentlemen, the cost."

To press each for his share was labour lost :

And much less could he force the banded throng :

Against a troop was ever one man strong ?

Upon the door-step stay'd the fellow-guest,

Without a word, but still with look deprest.

The landlord now despair'd to see his own :

And "Truth, where art thou?" cried in heighten'd tone.

She answer'd : "Here, good sir, but what to do

" I knew not : till I met yon reckless crew,

" My want of food was wholly unsupplied ;

" Ay, and without them, I had long since died."

XXXII.

THE LION AND THE GOAT.
(P. F. 253.)

A LION met a goat, beside a spring,

In summer thirst to all brings suffering,

To beasts, and soil, and plants, no less than man.

For the first sip a quarrel then began.

Dire was the strife, and would have led to death,

But that they parted, to recover breath

For further conflict, just a little space,

Looking each other fiercely in the face :

And gathering vultures suddenly they spied,

Which, from aloft, their wrathful struggle eyed,

In expectation of a well-timed treat,

Since he that fell would furnish dainty meat.

Now, as on these the weary champions gaze,

" Come, cease we fighting," each to other says ;

" Better be friends, than yield the vultures food !"

By thee, my son, too, be dire strife eschew'd,

For homes and cities it hath ever strew'd.

XXXIII.

THE CROW AND THE SWAN.
(P. F. 206.)

A CROW the swans their fair complexion grudged :

He would have been quite as white-skinn'd, he
>   judged,

Did he but float on river, or on lake :

He left the hearths, where he was wont to take

His food, and to the swans' dank dwelling went.

To him no change of hue ablution lent,

But famine kill'd him, when no food he got.

Nature a change of dwelling alters not.

XXXIV.

THE DOG AND THE COCKLE.
(P. F. 223.)

To swallow eggs was a dog's wonted fun :
Seeing a cockle, this he took for one,
And gorged it with a gulp immediately :
Then sorely griped in bowels by and by,
" A just reward," quoth he, "my sin hath found,
" Because for eggs I took whate'er was round."

Choose thou the real, not what fair may sound.

XXXV.

THE BULL, THE LIONESS, AND THE WILD BOAR.
(P. F. 395.)

A BULL a lion wrapt in slumber caught,
Whose death by goring with his horns he wrought ;
His dam came up, and o'er her cub made wail :
A wild boar overheard her piteous tale.

Standing afar,—"How many more," quoth he,

" Of mothers weep for offspring bitterly,

" Which having slaughter'd, ye your banquet keep."

Know that ill-doers their deserts shall reap.

XXXVI.

THE GNAT AND THE LION.
(P. F. 234.)

A BOASTING gnat drew to a lion near ;

And said : " No greater strength for me to fear

" Hast thou ! What is thy force ?—with claws to
   scratch,

" With teeth to bite ?—this might a woman match :

" Nay, oft she does, when striving with her mate

" For no great ends. My strength is far more great.

" But come ! let us the strength of each compare !"

It buzz'd, and fixed on parts devoid of hair,

And the poor lion's face and nostrils stung.

That lion's claws to his own visage clung,

Reeking with blood.   He yielded in despair.

Then the gnat's trumpet sounded triumph rare.

It flew aloft, in lion-victor's pride,

Till, captured in a spider's web, it cried,

" Alas my wretched fate, since e'en tho' I

" The greatest conquer, by the small I die!"

Weakness 'gainst strength may something seem to do,

Yet pays the cost to foes it never knew.

XXXVII.

THE SWALLOW AND THE CROW.
'P. F. 416.)

A TWITTERING swallow hail'd a husky crow.

" Me for a royal maid of Athens know !

" And as a daughter of her kings of yore :

" Not small renown our house of heroes bore."

To this vague prattle (love of talk was strong :)

She adds the tale of Tereus, and his wrong.

These words to her the crow in answer said :

" Pandion's boastful child, Athenian maid !

" Had you a tongue, to what lengths would you go,

" Since, when it is cut off, you twitter so !"

XXXVIII.

THE GULL AND THE KITE.
(P. F. 239.)

A GULL once gorged a fish, fell down, and died,

Because its throat to pass the spoil denied.

A kite looked on, and said : " Just fate ensues,

" Since, though a fowl, a fishy food you choose."

Aim your own station, and no more, to fill.

Work nature's hests, and you escape from ill.

XXXIX.

THE HORSE AND THE STAG.

(P. F. 175. ARISTOT. RHET. II. 20.)

At summer season, o'er a flowery mead
A well maned horse was wont at large to feed;
And ill brook'd he that any other beast
Should graze the herbage, where he loved to feast.
For his sole use he deemed the meads unfold
Their verdure.   But a stag, not over bold,
Came oft, and nibbled at the grassy plain;
So how to punish her he wrack'd his brain.
Seeing a man, he ask'd his sage advice,
Who said that he would help him in a trice
To take upon the stag a vengeance just,
If to the bridle he his mouth would trust,
And on his saddled back the man might ride.
The horse—a slave since then till now—complied.

Observe, I pray, the grievous curse entail'd,
Where selfishness has over sense prevail'd.

XL.

THE LION, THE WOLF, AND THE FOX.

(P. F. 255.)

A LION sick within his cave reclined ;

Then came each beast of all the savage kind

To visit and enquire for their king.

Beyond the rest the fox kept loitering.

Now, the wolf fixt on this auspicious time

Slily to charge the fox with treason's crime,

" Since she alone with negligence did treat

" The king of brutes, to which the earth is meat,

" When she to ease his sufferings should be near,

" As wise in counsel, and in judgment clear :"—

Up came the fox, as the wolf closed his speech,

And his last words chanc'd Reynard's ears to reach.

The lion shook his mane in angry mood,

To see the fox into his cave intrude ;

But the sagacious fox was nowise cowed,

And only pray'd for right of speech allowed.

'Twas granted.   Then said she (the wolf stood near):

" Now who, my liege, of beasts assembled here,

" Hath render'd thee such loyal aid as I ?

" I have the country traversed low and high,

" And question'd every leech concerning thee,

" In hopes some one might point a remedy ;

" Aye and I've found, nor vainly sought, the way :

" Physicians learnèd by experience say,

" That hence the patient certain ease shall win,

" If from a living wolf he strip the skin,

" And this, yet warm, around his body wrap."

He said.   Forthwith the wolf, that plann'd a trap,

Lay dead ; and thus the debt of malice paid.

" O wolf, ill-fated !" Reynard laughing said,

" 'Twas better that thou shouldst not counsel ill

" The lion, but guide right his kindly will :

" For whoso against others brings about

" Evil, the same shall turn and find him out."

XLI.

THE LION, PROMETHEUS, AND THE ELEPHANT.
(P. F. 261.)

THE lion urged it as a constant charge

Against Prometheus, that while fine and large

He made him, and with teeth had arm'd his jaw,

Fencing withal each foot with horny claw,

And rank'd him first of brutes for valour's praise,

" Such though I am, the cock my soul dismays,"

Quoth he.   Prometheus made him this reply:

" Pray, why on me should idle censure lie ?

" All I could give thou hast, as it was fit ;

" But if at times thy spirit quails a whit,

" No marvel !   In nought else thou fallest short."

So when Prometheus gave him this retort,

The lion bitterly his fate bemoan'd,

And his own cowardice, condemning, own'd.

He cared no more to live in such disgrace,

But, in this mind, encounter'd face to face

An elephant, with which to talk he stay'd.

Seeing its ears were hither thither sway'd,

He asked, " Why thus in motion keep your ears ?

" What beast, good sir, so dread to you appears,

" As thus your hearing-organs to confound ?"

It chanced a gnat buzz'd presently around :

" Seest thou yon buzzing mite ?" the huge beast said,

" Let it once pierce mine ear, and I am dead."

The lion, hearing this, took heart to cry,

" Why should I any more desire to die,

" Since better far than elephants am I ?

" And as much better in my lot have fared,

" As cock beats gnat, when both have been compared."

None are unblest, save by comparison :

This is a wise saw, and an ancient one.

XLII.

THE PEACOCK AND THE CRANE.

(P. F. 397. Compare Part I. LXV.)

THE fine-helm'd peacock and the Libyan crane
Were wont to pasture on one grassy plain.
Long time in mutual amity they passed,
But dire contention made them foes at last,
And golden plumage strove with ashen hue,
To which a good complexion's meed was due.
Jibes at the crane the grinning peacock throws,
And mocks its colour with uplifted nose ;
Claiming his own "to be the perfect wing
" Of gold and purple, worthy of a king."
To whom the crane a fitting answer made :
" And yet 'tis I who cloud-capp'd heights pervade ;
" Nighest the shining stars my notes are heard,
" While you are but a weak and slow-paced bird,
" That skim the ground, nor ever upward go ;
" But, like a bantam-cock, mid chickens crow."

Fame, tho' I threadbare went, I'd covet most :

Riches, with name unknown, on me were lost.

XLIII.

THE WOLF AND THE ASS.

(P. F. 281.)

A WOLF, whom fellow wolves to lead them chose,

Would fain to all an equal law propose,

That whatsoe'er each took in foraging,

To share amongst his fellows he should bring.

An ass heard this, and bristling up his mane,

To the fair dealer spoke in laughing strain :

" Well have you said, intending laws to frame

" To govern wolves.　But tell me how you came

" In a sly corner of your lair to lay

" Apart the feast, which you stole yesterday ?"

XLIV.

THE WOLF AND THE LION.
(P. F. 280.)

In desert spots a wolf had chanced to roam,

And, when the day-star near'd its western home,

Seeing his shadow long and tall appear,

Said, " Being larger, need I lions fear?

" Sure, to a hundred feet in measure grown,

" I shall be lord of all, not brutes alone !"

Upon th' exulting wolf a lion sprung,

And seized and ate him.   The confession wrung

From his last utterance was, " My cause of doom

" Is, that on self-opinion I presume."

XLV.

THE WOLF AND THE SHEEP.
(P. F. 285.)

BITTEN by dogs, a wolf lay sick and sore,
And of a passing sheep began to implore
Relief for thirst.   A spring of water flow'd
Hard by.   Then said he, " Were there but bestow'd
" By thee a draught of this, my thirst to slake,
" To furnish mine own meat I'd undertake."
" I give thee drink ! then I should be thy meat ! "
The sheep replied.

    Fly foes that use deceit.

XLVI.

THE JACKDAW AND THE CROWS.
(P. F. 201.)

A DAW in size his fellows much surpass'd,
So on his tribe a scornful glance he cast,
And chose to be a tribesman of the crows.
He therefore sought their presence, to propose
Dwelling with them, and clubbing for his food.
His form they neither knew, nor understood
His accents, with his race in unison ;
So, beating him, they made him quick begone.
Driven from these, he sought his own again ;
But they, at his desertion in disdain—
Because they thought his conduct insolent—
To take him back by no means would consent.
An outlaw'd, homeless daw was he from thence.

None will attain with strangers influence.

XLVII.

THE FLIES.

(P. F. 293.)

On honey in a storeroom spilt, some flies
Began to feast in gathering companies.
The sweet repast their lingering wills detain'd,
And as their feet were by its pow'r constrain'd,
Upon the wing no longer could they rise ;
Then, as they choke, each one to other cries,
" Alas ! poor creatures, down our lives we lay,
" Most sadly by brief pleasure led astray."

XLVIII.

THE MOON AND ITS MOTHER.

(P. F. 389.)

The moon her lady mother once besought,
That a close-fitting tunic might be wrought
For her.   To whom her mother, smiling, said,
" How shall a dress be wrought or measurèd

" For thy uncertain figure ? over-great

" Now, near the full ; and then in bursting state ;

" Gibbous and crescent-shaped thou wilt be soon.

" All through the month come changes of the moon."

XLIX.

THE MOUSE AND THE FROG.

(P. F. 298.)

A FIELD-MOUSE to a frog, by evil lot,

Became a friend, and hence destruction got ;

For with the field-mouse first they came to eat,

And then resorted to the frog's retreat.

But evil soon became the frog's design.

He tied his friend's foot to him with a line,

And dragg'd him to the margin of a lake,

A bath within its marshy depths to take :

Drown'd by the waters thus, the mouse was choked,

And perish'd, to a frog by being yoked.

Its corpse then as the eddying surface bore,

A hawk with eager talons upward tore,

With it was dragg'd the frog, to which 'twas tied :
Doom'd for the hawk two banquets to provide,
He learn'd what wages want of thought betide.

L.

THE SPENDTHRIFT AND THE SWALLOW.

(P. F. 304.)

To a young spendthrift but one garb was left,
Of all but this by reckless waste bereft.
He saw a swallow, out of season, fly
Near him, and heard its little twittering cry.
Thinking at once that the spring-tide was near,
Of parting with his coat he had no fear ;
And so he took and sold it, like the rest :
But soon, when winter storms about her prest,
And suddenly the strong wind round her roll'd,
Alas ! the wretched swallow died of cold.
Her for a while the young man looked upon,
And said, " Poor bird, much evil hast thou done !

" Appearing ere the spring-tide, thou hast wrought

" Ruin to me, and to thyself, for nought."

Evil is wastefulness and want-of-thought.

LI.

See Part I. 128.

LII.

See Part I. 124.

LIII.

THE SHEEP AND THE DOG.

(P. F. 317. Compare Fragment 1, Part I.)

A SHEEP one day address'd its shepherd thus :

" You shear our fleece, and keep it, shorn, from us ;

" You drain our milk, and press it, if you choose :

" Our young to swell your flock we ne'er refuse.

" For us nought else you do, but simply lead

" To pasture. All the grass, on which we feed,

" Is found for you by kind, all-nursing earth.

" E'en on the hills a fruitful soil gives birth

" For you, without your help, to verdure new,

" Beneath moist air, and soft descending dew.

" Yet while such profit from us you derive,

" Still you would have your dog among us thrive,

" Feeding it, as yourself, on best of food."

The dog was near and heard. These words ensued :

" O, thou that bleatest foolish-minded talk,

" Were it not that I oft amidst you walk,

" Abundant herbage you no more would eat,

" But be to brutes, that roam the hills, a treat.

" Now running all around you, timid sheep

" From busy thief, and ravening wolf I keep."

To thankless men this fable is addrest,

Who benefactors with ill-names molest.

LIV.

See Part I. 125.

LV.

THE ASS AND THE FOX.
(P. F. 325.)

An ass was fond of eating prickly food,

And grinning Reynard ask'd, when this she view'd,

" With tongue so soft, how is it, best of brutes,

" That on hard food you live, and thorny fruits?

" How can your tongue from prickly wounds escape?"

To babblers well this fable thou may'st shape.

LVI.

THE ASS WEARING THE LION'S SKIN.

(P. F. 333.)

In lion's skin an ass once went about,

And threw the brute creation into rout ;

They thought him a true lion, not an ass :

He therefore tried, when Reynard chanced to pass,

If, like the rest, a fox would yield to fright.

But when he met that wily creature's sight

(Now she, by chance, that moment heard him bray),

Quoth she to him, " Be sure of what I say,

" Had I not just now mark'd you when you bray'd,

" I, like my fellow-brutes, had been afraid."

LVII.

AN ASS CARRYING AN IMAGE.

(P. F. 324.)

A COUNTRYMAN had placed upon his ass
An image ; and, in driving, made him pass
Right through a village.   All men homage paid
Unto the idol.   Then the ass betray'd
Elation, thought himself a god, and felt
That 'twas to his divinity they knelt.
Pricking his ears, with an astounding bray,
He presently declined the onward way ;
At seeing which his driver angry grew,
And with a stick compell'd him to pursue
His journey.   " Thou art but an ass," said he,
" Though on thy back there rides divinity."

LVIII.

THE BIRD-CATCHER AND THE LARK.
(P. F. 340.)

A BIRD-CATCHER, while he his springes set,
Was by a lark, that saw him, quickly met.
" What dost thou here, so busy on the ground ?"
Quoth he, " A first-rate city this, I found !"
He went and hid himself when this was said.
Straight came the lark, by his false words misled,
In haste at once to plant its colony :
And in the toils was caught unwittingly.
Up ran the bird-catcher to seize his prey;
Then did the captive to its captor say,
" If cities such as these, good sir, you plant,
" The list of dwellers in them will be scant."

Cities and homes are most made desolate,
When evil heads have care of their estate.

LIX.

THE TAIL AND MEMBERS OF A SERPENT.

(P. F. 344.)

A SERPENT'S tail once claim'd the lead to take,

And drag the other members in its wake.

Then did the body it, as mad, oppose :

" How wilt thou lead us without eyes or nose ?

" Unlike the rest of beasts, that roam a-field."

In vain. The thinking limbs were forced to yield.

So the tail led the rest with senseless sway,

And blindly dragg'd the body every way.

It fell at last into a cleft of rock,

Whence back, head, body, met a fearful shock.

Then fawningly it did the head beseech :

" Save, mistress, save me, pray, from danger's reach,

" For of bad judgment now I reap the fruit."

This fable to a commons best will suit

Which, frensied and perverted, fain would rise

And hold dominion over men more wise.

LX.

THE FARMER AND THE SERPENT.
(P. F. 96.)

A SNAKE, that by a farmer's door did hide,
Stung his child's foot, and so the infant died.
Great was the sorrow which the parents bore.
And the sire, smitten by a blow so sore,
Taking a stone, approach'd the serpent's den,
Waiting to kill it coming forth again.
Out from its hole it came to hunt for prey :
Up ran in eager haste the sire straightway,
And at it with main force he cast a stone,
Which lack'd success, to little purpose thrown ;
His aim to hurt the murderous snake did fail,
Further than, at its end, to bruise its tail.
Then fearful lest the reptile him should slay,
And thus the fracture of that tail repay,
Honey and meal and water he procured,
And thus his foe to be at peace adjured.

But then the monster, hissing from its hole

(To which, when wounded, it for shelter stole),

Some such defiance at the father threw :

" Till *you* the tomb, the stone *I* cease to view,

" There never can be peace betwixt us two."

LXI.

THE BOY HUNTING LOCUSTS.

(P. F. 350.)

To gather locusts forth a lad had gone,

He caught a host, ere he set eyes upon

A scorpion.   Thinking this a locust, he

Hollow'd his hand, and stretch'd it eagerly

To grasp his prize.   The reptile saw the lad

Was guileless, and with him this converse had :

" Boy, get thee gone, nor hands upon me lay !

" For, catching me, thou'lt cast thine all away."

LXII.

THE YOUNG THIEF AND HIS MOTHER.
(P. F. 351.)

A BOY from school purloin'd a comrade's slate,

And to his mother bore his prize, elate.

She took it, did not say his act was wrong,

Or warn his hands from what did not belong

To them.   Ere long the youth had learn'd to thieve,

And would not, untouched, things more precious leave.

The wonted habit soon became a trade :

Then, in the act of sacrilege way-laid

And caught, with hands behind him bound he went

The road the lawless are with hangmen sent.

With tears and moans his mother went behind,

And her son begg'd the hangmen to be kind,

And to him this one favour to accord,

To breathe within her ear some latest word.

Ready to list, she near her offspring drew,

Who violently bit her ear in two.

When she deplored such treatment from her child,

And the bystanders' language was not mild

In blame of one whose acts so impious proved

Towards her that bare him ; " Surely it behoved

" Her, first and foremost," said he, "to deter

" My youth from theft. I owe my wreck to her.

" 'Twas she who welcomed first the stolen slate.

" 'Tis she conducts me now to Pluto's gate."

LXIII.

THE COCKLES.

(P. F. 214.)

A-ROASTING cockles, said a farmer's son,

When they to hiss and bubble had begun,

" Ye senseless creatures, that, with homes on fire,

" Strike up a tuneful strain, and join in choir."

LXIV.

PROMETHEUS AND MANKIND.
(P. F. 383.)

PROMETHEUS erst, when Jove the order spake,
Proceeded men and brutes, 'tis said, to make.
But when Jove saw that beasts outnumbered men,
He bade him mix some of the brutes again,
And fashion them into the human mould.
The brutes into a lump Prometheus rolled,
And form'd men of it, e'en as Jove desired.
But, as for those so moulded, it transpired
That in the change they gained a human shape,
Yet did not from their earlier mind escape ;
But kept that to the end, which they began
By sharing with the brutes and not with man.

LXV.

THE THIRSTY PIGEON.

(P. F. 357.)

A THIRSTY pigeon on a sign-board spied
A cup of water, at mid summer-tide.
Taking the picture for the actual thing,
She bore down on it with a rustling wing.
Unwittingly against the board she dash'd,
And fell to earth with wings and feathers smash'd ;
The cat at once an easy prey secured.

Rush upon nought, with purpose unmatured,
If passion guides, quick ruin is ensured.

LXVI.

THE MAN AND THE PARTRIDGE.
(P. F. 356.)

A SPORTSMAN in his net a partridge caught,
To sup on which immediately he thought :
But for her life entreating mournfully
She cried, " Oh spare, and do not slaughter me,
" And I for thee a crowd of birds will get,
" Decoying ready victims to thy net."
Said he, "Thou silly partridge, stay thy cry ;
" It is for this cause chiefly thou shalt die,
" That never more thou may'st betray thy friends."

Evil design'd for others ever tends
To thine own hurt.   And so doth ev'ry plan
Thy malice plots against a fellow-man.

LXVII.

THE BAT AND THE CAT.
(P. F. 307).

THAT foe to every feathered fowl, the cat,
Caught, as it lay upon the ground, a bat ;
Which, fearing instant doom without delay,
Endeavour'd thus with pray'rs her fate to stay :
" Oh, do not slaughter me, good cat," said she,
" No living thing hath e'er found hurt from me.
" I in the daylight never quit my nest :
" When beasts go out to hunt, I take my rest,
" But forth at moonless dusk I alway fare,
" To get my food in dew-encumber'd air."
The cat then answer'd thus : " As I'm a foe
" To birds in general, can I let thee go ? "
" I am no bird," was next the bat's reply :
" Four-footed, fed on bloodless food am I."
On hearing this the cat its prey resign'd.
'Twas saved from no small peril, soon to find

Another captor of the feline brood,

Which thought to take it, like a mouse, for food.

But then she pray'd and said, "No mouse was
    she,

"For she had wings, and wing'd no mouse could
    be :"

Thus came she out of double danger free.

LXVIII.

THE TORTOISE AND THE HARE.

(P. F. 420.)

To the shy hare the tortoise smiling spoke,

When he about her feet began to joke :

" I'll pass thee by, though fleeter than the gale."

" Pooh !" said the hare, " I don't believe thy tale."

" Try but one course, and thou my speed shalt
    know."

" Who'll fix the prize, and whither we shall go ? "

Of the fleet-footed hare the tortoise asked.

To whom he answer'd, " Reynard shall be tasked

" With this ; that subtle fox, whom thou dost see."

The tortoise then (no hesitater she !)

Kept jogging on, but earliest reached the post ;

The hare, relying on his fleetness, lost

Space, during sleep, he thought he could recover

When he awoke.   But then the race was over ;

The tortoise gain'd her aim, and slept *her* sleep.

From negligence doth care the vantage reap.

LXIX.

THE ROSE AND THE AMARANTH.

(P. F. 384.)

An amaranth had sprung up near a rose,

And said, " Than thee no flower more comely grows,

" Long'd for by gods, and dear to man, as well.

" I count thee blest both for thy fragrant smell,

" And lovely beauty."   Then the rose replied,

" Good amaranth, 'tis vain the truth to hide :

" For me the threads of life are quick outspun ;

" For if not pluck'd, I soon am all undone

" By withering.   But thou dost alway bloom,

" And living, ever-green, escape the tomb."

May a fixt lot (no matter small or great)

Be rather mine, than high but changeful state.

LXX.

THE SHEPHERD AND THE WOLF.

(P. F. 374.)

A WOLF'S young cub was by a shepherd caught.

This, with his dogs to nurture, home he brought.

In time it grew up, in the sheepfold rear'd,

Where if so be another wolf appear'd,

Intent to rob of lamb or kid the fold,

First rank among the dogs would this one hold,

Quickest the daring robber to pursue.

But if the dogs of chasing weary grew,

And toward the sheepcot, failing to o'ertake

The spoiler, chanced their backward road to make,

Not, as in chase, the tame wolf onward went,

But for a share fell in by accident.

Or, should no other wolf, to steal a sheep,

Chance from outside into the fold to leap,

Then with the dogs he made a sly repast

On one.   The shepherd caught the rogue at last,

And from a tree, to kill him, let him swing.

Good habits do not from ill natures spring.

LXXI.

THE OLIVE AND THE FIG-TREE.
(P. F. 124.)

Olive and Fig-tree strove for beauty's prize.

" At no time," said the first, " my foliage dies,'

" But the fig's bloom is put forth, once for all,

" At one set season, and is then but small."

So then to her the fig-tree made reply :

" Nay ! but when snows fall from the wintry sky,

" And settle in thy leaves, still in their bloom,

" Thy beauteous freshness doth but bring thee doom.

" Whereas, on finding me of foliage quit,

" Snow falls to earth.   I am unhurt by it."

To man's disgrace tends beauty void of wit.

LXXII.

THE PARD AND THE FOX.

(P. F. 42.)

ONCE did a spotted pard to boast begin

Of all the brute-kind the most various skin,

To whom said Reynard : " Be it so ! Yet I

" Possess a mind of more variety

" Than thy skin or thy mind."

Each magnifies

That which within his own possession lies.

LXXIII.

THE FOX AND THE HEDGEHOG.

(P. F. 36.   ARISTOT. RHET. II. 20.)

ÆSOP in Samos to a chief, his friend,

Upon his trial, wishing aid to lend—

This chief was of the wealthiest in the isle—

With this apt fable did the mob beguile.

Crossing a rapid stream a fox one day
By the tide's violence was borne away
Into the deep gorge of a rocky hole,
There falling down she lay, poor fainting soul,
Wholly unable from her place to move,
And long with her sad plight but feebly strove.
Then upon her a swarm of dog-ticks burst,
Craving for food, to suck her blood athirst.
But a stray hedgehog spied her troubled state,
And, to her sufferings compassionate,
Ask'd, runs the story, "If her wish would be
" The dog-ticks' slaughter?" " By no means," said she,
" I pray you by the Nymphs, this swarm disperse."
" Why would you not be rid of such a curse ?"
The hedgehog asked again. " Because e'en now
" These in each vein are full of blood, I trow !"
Replied sly Reynard, " What they drain is slight.
" Get rid of these when full, and you invite
" Others to come, a famine-wasted force,
" And wholly suck my blood without remorse."

LXXIV.

THE SOW AND THE BITCH.
(P. F. 409.)

THE sow and bitch betwixt them held dispute
Which was best breeder. Said the sow, "No brute
" With four legs bears more quick than I, you'll find."
" Yes," said the bitch, " but then your whelps are
blind."

LXXV.

THE SOW AND THE BITCH.
(P. F. 408.)

A sow and bitch each other did revile.
The first, by her who guards Cythera's isle,
Sware with her teeth the other's bones to break.
The bitch then mock'd the thought a sow should take
An oath by Venus, as her favourite.
" That thou shouldst swear by Venus, sure, is fit !

" For thou, 'tis plain, by her art most beloved,

" Seeing that she hath from her fane removed

" Farthest the men that make a meal of pork."

Then grunts the sow, whose wits were all at work :

" Learn thou that it from this is chiefly seen,

" How much beloved I am by beauty's queen ;

" For hating him that seeks to do me hurt,

" Or dares to kill me, him she doth avert.

" But thou hast an ill-savour, live or dead."

A man of sense converts whate'er is said

By evil speakers, mockery to raise,

Through skilful handling into real praise.

LXXVI.

GOODS AND EVILS.

(P. F. 1.)

EVILS once thrust the blessings all away

From their free sojourn midst the sons of clay.

For hosts of evils had the earth possest.

Then did the blessings soar to Heaven, in quest

Of satisfaction on th' usurping race,

Nor deign'd with such to tarry in one place.

In blending them Nature had been to blame !

How could they mix, if, evermore the same,

Jarring and quick-to-clash are man's affairs ?

To fix their rule, to Jove they lift their pray'rs.

Jove's fiat was : " Let ills be mixt below.

" Singly among men be it yours to go !"

Hence then it is, that ills in numbers run :

For they are join'd, and go not one by one.

But all good things come down from Jove to men,

Each to but one or two, and slowly then.

LXXVII.

THE CAMEL AND JUPITER.
(P. F. 184.)

GRUDGING a bull its horns the camel went,
Pray'rs for the like at Jove's throne to present.
Jove in disgust, because she wish'd for more,
Though she had a fine, stalwart frame before,
Not only gives no horns, but also shears,
To check her grasping, somewhat from her ears.

To seek what fate omits, unmeet appears.

LXXVIII.

THE DANCING MONKEYS.
(P. F. 360.)

To teach some apes bethought him Egypt's king
The Pyrrhic dance.   Of every living thing
Apes are most imitative.   What men do
Under their notice, they will copy too.

Dress'd then in bright and elegant array,

These famous maskers set about their play,

With many looking on.   Most gracefully

Awhile they acted : till a stander-by,

A fine smart fellow, from his vest let drop

Handfuls of nuts, and brought them to a stop.

These, spilt around, the apes no sooner view,

Than they cease dancing, tear their robes in two,

Smash all their masks, and rush on these amain,

Making their monkey-breeding vastly plain.

To change one's nature is but toil in vain.

LXXIX.

THE FOX AND THE GOAT.

(P. F. 45.)

A GOAT athirst, when it beheld a pool,

Descended a deep gorge, its heat to cool.

He drank, ere he discover'd how unwise

Was his descent.   Alone he could not rise

From out the pit.   He paused, look'd up, and sought

Assistance.   Thirst had just then Reynard brought

To pass the opening.   She the goat espied,

And ask'd him, if the stream a draught supplied.

" Ay ! and as clear as crystal !" answered he,

" But the hole's steep, its outlet hard to see."

The Fox then to the broad-beard made reply :

" Faint not at that : I look'd down from on high,

" And judg'd that thence 'twas easy to ascend.

" Come, make thine horns against the pit side bend,"

Thus said the Fox, " that I may come down so :

" Then running up I'll drag thee from below."

She came down, drank, and went up from the pit,

Yet, after all, help'd not the goat a bit.

And when he blamed her base ingratitude,

Then the fox made this observation rude :

" Nay ! if of sense you'd had as large a share,

" As you can boast a wavy beard of hair,

' Not without egress had you been down there."

LXXX.

THE BEES AND JUPITER.

(P. F. 287.)

THE Hymettian bee, a mother of the combs,

Once with a gift approach'd the heavenly homes,

Honey for Jove, fresh-gather'd from the hives,

Honey, in which o'er smoke and age survives

A flow'ry scent. Delighted with the gift

Jove sware to grant the pray'r she might uplift.

" Grant me a sting, that if by men," she said,

" Upon my combs a rifling hand be laid,

" I may, by stinging such, my hurters slay."

Angry was Jove to hear the insect pray

For man's destruction : yet, however loth,

He could but grant where he had pledged his oath.

The sting, however, which he gave, was such,

That when bees smite, they perish with the touch.

Her sting the life, that keeps her on the wing,

She leaves that life where'er she leaves her sting.

LXXXI.

THE SON AND THE FATHER.

(P. F. 349.)

A TIMID old man had a valiant boy,

And dream'd he saw a lion him destroy.

So fearing lest the dream should be fulfill'd,

A pleasant room for him he set to build :

And, as some solace for vexation sore,

Had wild beasts painted o'er each wall and door.

Among them was the lion's picture shown.

So when on this the young man's glance was thrown,

Rage and chagrin more fiercely on him press'd,

And standing near, the lion he addrest :

" O worst of brutes, because my father's eye

" In dreamy sleep did once behold a lie,

" I am thus idly prison'd for a dream.

" On thee what vengeance shall sufficient seem ?"

Threatening the lion with his words so grand,

The young man through a panel thrust his hand,

To break a splint from a bush near the wall,

Meaning to burn the lion as tinder small:

But as the prickles chanced to wound his thumb,

Quick was the swelling to his waist to come.

Opprest with wracking pain the young man lay,

And soon his anguish took his speech away:

O'er Acheron's stream, poor wretch, another fare.

What fate allots thee, be resign'd to bear.

Nor seek by shifts thy destiny to cheat.

For what must come, 'tis best a man should meet.

·

LXXXII.

THE WILD BOAR AND THE FOX.

(P. F. 407.)

A WILD boar once stood at an old tree's foot,

Whetting his tusks. The query Reynard put:

What fancy led him thus his tusks to whet,

No risk being near, no hunter to beset

His path—in fact, no need.   The boar replied,
" I, like a fool, should wretchedly have died
" Oft, had I sought arms but when danger prest."

Man's life is all a plot.   Be ready, lest
Evil befall.   Precaution's ever best.

LXXXIII.

THE LIONESS AND THE BEASTS.
(P. F. 240.)

AN answer to the quadrupeds once came,
That put their boasts of fruitfulness to shame.
In truth they went and tax'd the lioness,
Wishing against her to prove barrenness.
" Come tell thou us, how many cubs dost bear ?"
She smiled, and met them with this answer rare,
" But one, yet he is thoroughbred all o'er."

Than hosts of fools one man of sense is more.

LXXXIV.

THE BALD RIDER.

(P. F. 410.)

A BALD man in a wig did ride a race :
A sudden gust dislodged it from its place.
It flew aloft, by breezy motion borne,
And the by-standers laugh'd the man to scorn.
But said the bald-head, as he ceased to ride,
" What marvel if strange locks refused to bide
" Where mine own hair had long deserted me ?"

Vexed at the loss of goods let no man be :
For borrowers of this life's things are we.

LXXXV.

THE CRANE AND THE FOX.

(P. F. 34.)

THE Libyan crane and shameless fox agreed
That each by turns would with the other feed.
Sly Reynard only set some greasy broth
Before her guest, pour'd on a broad plate forth ;
And bade her of the feast to take her fill.
Much fun she caused, as evermore her bill
With useless toil she struck against the ware,
Whilst of the broth it failed to gain a share.
The Libyan bird then sought to entertain
The roguish fox, and play the host would fain.
Of barley-meal a thin-necked jar was full,
And out of this *her* bill, thrust in, could pull
Enough of food.   So now the laugh had she
At Reynard, who stood gaping hungrily.
The fox's snout would not the jar-neck fit.

For what you do to others, they'll be quit.

LXXXVI.

THE HUSBANDMAN AND THE LICE.
(P. F. 411.)

A PLOUGHMAN was half eaten up by lice.

Leaving his plough, he shook his garment twice.

When a third time they bit him shamelessly,

Wishing by all means of them to get free,

Lest cleanliness should loss-of-work require,

He doff'd his clothes, and threw them on the fire.

I would not have him thrice from fire abstain,

Who twice hath lost his wits by woman's bane.

P

LXXXVII.

THE BRAZIER AND HIS DOG.
(P. F. 413.)

A BRAZIER in his house a pet-dog kept ;
And while the master forged, the spaniel slept ;
But when the master dined, he rose from sleep,
A fawning watch for scraps and bones to keep.
The man once shook his staff in angry mood,
And said, " Most wretched of the canine brood,
" What shall I do with such a slumbering cur,
" From laziness so strong, so hard to stir ?
" Dost thou not know that toil alone doth send
" Gifts that are good ? "

　　　　　　　　　　I'd have thee, without end,
An idler's ears with this sound warning fill ;
'Tis idleness that makes a man fare ill.

LXXXVIII.

THE HUSBANDMAN AND THE VIPER.
(P. F. 97.)

It happen'd to a labourer to behold
A viper frozen by excessive cold,
At winter, in the fields.   By pity press'd,
He lifted it and placed it in his breast,
Hoping to kindle vital warmth anew.
Away the viper, quick reviving, threw
Its numbness, and the friendly rustic stung,
Who said, a-dying, as from him he flung
The snake : "I spared the wretch.   My doom is
      meet.
"When whole, I should have crush'd it 'neath my
      feet."

LXXXIX.

WINTER AND SPRING.

(P. F. 414.)

Hoar Winter strung these words, to jeer at Spring:

" To none doth thine appearance quiet bring.

" One to the groves, to fields another hies

'' In haste, or where the woodland valley lies.

" To such the choicest early flowers are treats,

'' Lilies, or roses ever-breathing sweets,

" They cull to glad the eye, the wreath to twine:

'' These gifts hath Spring. But these are less than

  mine.

'' For I, who ride upon the sea-dash'd prows,

" Disturb the waves, the stormy wind arouse.

'' By me the rains and frozen hails are brought;

" And lumps of snow to icy substance wrought:

" So that all tarry, while I last, at home,

" At hearth or board, and do not care to roam;

" But revel in the sweet sound of the lyre,

" Strains of melodious song, and youthful choir.

" These are all Winter's makeweights, you must know !

" And granted that delight and praises flow

" From men's lips at thy name ; yet while I shed

" Charms o'er men's homes, my name is cherishèd

" By those who rightly judge, as sweet of sound."

For thine, o'er strange goods, claim not higher
          ground ;

For e'en in these some beauty may be found.

XC.

THE SWALLOWS AND THE SWANS.

(P. F. 416.)

GIBES at the snow-white swans the swallows threw,

Because they from men's company withdrew,

But loved to hover round the meads, and bide

By the marsh-pools, and by the river side,

Delighting most of all to dwell apart,

And keep remote from crowds their tuneful art.

" Our charm is in great cities, men and all,

" In roof, and chamber, corridor and hall,"

Thus said the swallows, "And we chirp our tale

" Most sweetly ; yea, the old establish'd wail

" Babbled from ancient days to th' Attic race,

" Of Athens and Pandion, Tereus, Thrace,

" Exile and marriage, mutilated tongue,

" Wrongs, writing-tablets, Itys slaughter'd young :

" How we had long a shape with men the same,

" But then, by transformation, birds became."

More said the Attic maids in such-like strain,

Yet did the swans to answer scarcely deign,

Nor then till late.   They hated wordy tales.

Their answer giv'n, of wit in no way fails.

" Oh, prating children of Athenian birth,

" All men would seek lone corners of the earth,

" From love of song, with gladness for our sakes,

" When Zephyr, blowing soft and sweetly, makes

" Our wings relax, and idly catch the breeze ;

" For such would list to honied melodies.

" Therefore it is we sing some trifling song :

" Albeit afar from every human throng,

" And that but rarely.   'Tis our fairest boast

" That measure in our strains we study most,

" Nor let our muses mingle with the crowd.

" But that of *you* men weary 'tis allowed,

" Nor will your nearness calmly tolerate ;

" For your unmeasured twittering they hate.

" Yet in all this ye suffer but your due,

" Since with your tongues cut out, 'twere well ye
       knew

" The charm of silence, and your prate gave o'er

" Of shameful wrongs, which in the house ye bore.

" But, not the less, ye babble most of all,

" Yet no melodious utterance let fall ;

" For ever is the maimèd tongue deplored,

" And Itys slain by Zethus with the sword."

XCI.

THE TWO POTS.

(P. F. 422.)

A RIVER on its stream two pots convey'd :
One was of brass, and one of clay was made.
The latter to the former, floating nigh,
Cried, " Float afar, and do not sail hard by :
" For if you nearer draw, I'm sure to break."

A poor man's house is very apt to shake,
When men of greater power are dwelling near,
And injury from them may fairly fear.

XCII.

THE FLEA AND THE WRESTLER.
(P. F. 424, *b.*)

UPON a wrestler's foot once perch'd a flea.
He moved.   It hopp'd and bit him sturdily.
Then was he wroth, and fain would it secure ;
Again it hopp'd, and got off safe and sure.
The wrestler worried, though by bites of fleas,
Cried groaning, " Wilt not aid me, Hercules ? "

It is mere insult to the Gods above
To pray them lesser evils to remove.

XCIII.

THE FLEA AND THE MAN.
(P. F. 424.)

A FLEA, which bit his foot, annoy'd a man.

He caught it, and to ask of it began,

"Who art thou, that thou dost so sharply bite,

"And puncture all my body with delight?"

Said it to him : "My life I thus sustain.

"Spare me : of no great harm can you complain."

And he in anger made it this reply,

"Therefore by these hands thou shalt straightway
        die.

"For what is evil, be it great or small,

"I would not have exist, to hurt at all."

XCIV.

THE FLEA AND THE OX.
(P. F. 426.)

ONCE of an ox a flea this question ask'd :

" Why do you bear by mortals to be task'd,

" And daily toil for them, since surely you

" Are a courageous brute, a fine one too ?

" Whereas I bite their flesh, though small to see,

" And fearless drink their red blood greedily."

The ox replied, " To men I know my debt.

" From them I ever care and kindness met.

" My forehead and my shoulders oft they stroke,

" And scratch and rub me, pleasure to provoke."

To the strong ox the flea then answer made,

" Ah ! but to luckless me this rubbing trade,

" You talk of, would result in death outright,

" Whene'er upon me men's nails chanced to light."

We ever love the hand that doth us good.

But requite hurt with hurt, in vengeful mood.

XCV.

THE ASS'S SHADOW.

(P. F. 339.)

A MAN of Athens on a summer's day,

To Megara was fain to make his way

On a pack-ass, he hired for a fixt sum.

So as he journey'd, when midday was come,

What time the sun pours down his beaming heat,

Under the ass's shade he sought retreat,

To shelter from the sun's excessive rays.

But the ass-driver now his right gainsays ;

" Th' agreement was for seat, and not for shade."

To which the other said, " that he had paid

" For the whole ass, and so its shadow bought."

So strifes about a shadow come to nought.

FINIS.

NOTES TO BABRIUS.

.

PART I.

PROEM II. 5.—Cybisas, or Cybissus. Theon and Apthonius, later teachers of rhetoric, mention Cybissus the Libyan, and Connis the Cilician, as fabulists. Cf. Muller and Donaldson, Gr. Lit. i. 193. Fables of the Phrygians, Cilicians, and Cyprians, are mentioned by Greek writers. See Bernhardy, Vol. I. p. 58.

FAB. XII.—This fable is based on the mythical story of Procne, Philomela, and Itys. The former of the sisters was transformed into a swallow, the latter into a nightingale. And the fable expresses the habits of each bird, the one building its nest near men's homes, and under their roofs, the other apart in far retreats. See Ov. Met. vi. 668. For a full account of the legend, the English reader may consult Grote's History of Greece, Vol. I. p. 269—271. Compare also Babrius, Part II. Fab. XXXVII. and Fab. XC. on the same subject.

IBID. v. 22.—Philomela's woes began after she had left Athens, on a visit to her sister Procne, whose husband Tereus conceived for her a fatal passion, which caused all the tragic tale, on which the Greek poets so much delight to dwell.

FAB. XXXI.—See preface with reference to the confusion

between αΐλουρος and γαλῆ, observable in Babrius and elsewhere. And see Notes and Queries, VoL VIII. p. 261—3. "The ancient names of the cat."

FAB. XXXII.—The Pleiads were the daughters (seven in number) of Atlas and Pleione. They were transformed into a cluster of stars at the back of Taurus, whose rising was in April or May, and their setting in November. Theocr. Id. xiii. 25. Virg. Georg. iv. 231. Hesiod (Works and Days, 384) places the time for ploughing at the season of their setting.

FAB. XLVI.—v. 9, 10. The stag was anciently supposed to be an exceedingly long lived animal ; but the opinion is confuted by Aristotle, H. A. vi. 29, and by later experience. It's life is at most from thirty-five to forty years in duration, according to Buffon and Cuvier.

FAB. LVIII.—In this fable Babrius follows the later version of the story of Pandora's Box, *i. e.* that it was full of *goods* not of *ills.* The old version is mentioned in Hesiod, Works and Days, 94—105. There, however, we read of Hope being left behind after the rest. As also, in Theognis, 1131—1146, we read of Hope remaining alone on earth, after Faith, and Modesty and the Graces had removed to Heaven.

FAB. LXIII.—Ancient writers, such as Xenocrates, Empedocles, and to a certain extent Plato, treat the remnants of the half wicked silver age as dæmons ; not good, as Hesiod held and represented them, but malignant and wicked. See Grote H. G. i. pp. 95—7. Ibid. 570—1, note. Here the heroes are confounded with these dæmons. Compare Plut. Quæst. Græc. c. vi. p. 292, where it appears that with the Locrians at Opus δαίμων was equivalent to ῞Hρως.

For the custom of wreathing the altars with fillets, alluded to in v. 3 of this fable, compare Theocr. Id. xxvi. 3—9, Horat. Od. iv. xi. 6, i. xix. 13. Virg. Ecl. viii. 64.

FAB. LXVI.—Babrius here adheres to the later fable, about Prometheus creating men, traces of which occur in Callimachus, and elsewhere. He places him among the Gods, but the Gods of the earliest period. For other fables in Babrius on the subject of Prometheus making man, see Part II, Fab. 64, which gives a similar version of the creation of man by him, to that of Horace, Od. i. xvi. 13, *Fertur Prometheus addere principi, &c.*

FAB. LXVIII. 4.—For the custom of placing the lots in a helmet, compare Hom. Il. vii. 176, where the lots are placed in Agamemnon's helmet, which is then shaken by Nestor.

IBID. 7.—The garden of Hesperus, or of the Hesperides, was in the more early writers placed at the remotest bound of the earth, afterwards at the extreme west, on the coast of Libya. Hesiod, Theog. 215, Plin. H. N. vi. 36, Virg. Æn. iv. 484, Ov. Met. iv. 632—8.

FAB. LXXI.—Compare Cicero Pro Cluentio, c. 49, Herodot. vii. 16.

FAB. LXXII. v. 6.—Grote, in his History of Greece, Vol. II. p. 289, remarks upon the inadequacy and irregularity of the supply of water in the low grounds of Greece. "Most of the rivers are torrents in the early spring, and dry before the end of summer. Rain runs off as rapidly as it falls, and springs are rare." Horace refers to this fable of the daw in his Epistles, i. iii. 18—20.

FAB. LXXXV.—Bergk, in a paper in the Classical Museum, Vol. iii. pp. 130—134, thinks that this fable, with its enumeration of Acarnanian, Dolopian, Molossian, Cretan dogs, &c. refers to the Achæan league, and to Aratus, as the Achæan dog chosen as the leader. He considers the wolves to be no other than the Ætolian league, and from this fable he gathers his chief argument for supposing King Alexander to be Alexander of Corinth and Nicæa.

FAB. XCV. 22.—Of the hatred of stags for all the serpent tribe, see Plin. Nat. His. viii. 50, xxii. 37, Ælian. N. A. II. 9.

Dioscorides De Mat. Med. III. 73, and Pliny l. c. state that serpents do not take hurt from the bites of serpents, if they feed on the plant "elaphoboscos"; and that the seed of this plant mixed with wine is a cure for the bites of serpents.

FAB. XCVIII.—Dubner and Lachmann agree in thinking the epimyth spurious here, and so does Sir G. C. Lewis. It is therefore not translated in this version. Eumenes exposed to the Macedonians the perfidy of his adversary's offers by quoting this fable. Cf. Thirlwall, Hist. Gr. vii. p. 273, 4.

FAB. CVII.—The epimyth of this fable has not been translated, because in addition to being judged to be spurious, it lacks point.

FAB. CVIII.—Compare Hor. Sat. II. vi. 79. See also Fab. XCIX above. As to the Camiræan fig mentioned in v. 25, see Smith's Dict. Gr. Rom. Geogr. Vol. I. pp. 713, 5. Camirus was a town of Rhodes, one of the three most ancient in the island, which was famous for its wine, raisins, and figs.

FAB. CXV. 7—Respecting the riches and vast commerce of the Red Sea, or Mare Erythræum, see Smith's Dict. Gr. Rom. Geogr. Vol II. 857, 8. See also the fabulist Avianus, Fab. II.

FAB. CXXV.—This fable should be carefully compared with the 54th fable in the second part of the original. The object of the translator has been to include in the 125th fable of this part, the result of a careful comparison of the two slightly differing texts. This fable is one which has been reduced to choliambic metres, from the prose MSS. of the Vatican, see F. De Furia, p. 150. Aristotle H. A. x. 6. mentions the Maltese dog, κυνίδιον Μελιταῖον.

FAB. CXXVIII.—This fable, like the 125th, had been restored to its metrical choliambic form before the discovery of the MS.

of Babrius. See the edition of F. De Furia, Fab. 365. The translation is based on a comparison of this fable and of fab. 51, in the second part.

FRAGM. I.—The same may be said here, as with reference to fables 125 and 128. The fragment is easy of completion if we compare with it Fab. 53, in Part II.

PART II.

PROEM. FAB. I.—For the murder of Æsop by the Delphians, who did not agree with him respecting the distribution of money among the citizens, with which he had been charged by Crœsus, see Plutarch de ser. Num. vind. p. 556. The Delphians repented, and granted compensation to his grandson. See Smith, D. G. R. B. vol. i. p. 47.[a]

FAB. II.—Cf. Aristoph. Av. 474.

FAB. V.—Compare Ovid. Fast. I. 357. See, too, Virg. Georg. II. 374—9.

FAB. XI.—Compare the slightly varied fable of Babrius, p. 1. Fab. 52.

FAB. XIII.—The Galli, or priests of Cybele, seem to have had their origin in Phrygia, and to have been chosen always from a poor and despised race of people; for while no other priests were allowed to beg, the Galli were permitted to do so on certain days. Compare Cicero de Leg. II. c. 9 and 16. Smith's Dict. G. R. A. 447.[a]

Ibid.—V. 6, 7. Atys or Attis was a beautiful shepherd of Phrygia, beloved by Cybele, whence arose all his misfortunes. See Ovid. Fast. iv. 221—44. His death was annually bewailed by the Galli. Compare the poem on the subject of Atys in

Catullus, LXIII.—These references will explain the allusions in the text of this fable.

FAB. XVI. 2.—A slight emendation of the Greek text suggests itself to the translator, viz. to read ἅσπερ for ὥσπερ, and to omit the comma after εἰώθει. This gives an intelligible sense to the passage, and facilitates translation. In the next fable verses 13—17 are evidently imperfect, and it is hopeless to attempt a literal translation. An approximatory guess is the translator's only resource.

FAB. XXII.—Compare with this fable that which occurs as Fable 71 of the first part. Sir G. C. Lewis illustrates the reply of the sea in v. 9—14, by a distich of Solon, from which it appears to have originated (p. 21, ed. Schneidewin), and by the speech of Artabanus to Xerxes, Herodot. vii. 16. In the last verse of the fable we would read,

τοῖς δρῶσιν οὐχὶ, τοῖσιν αἰτίοις μέμφου.

FAB. XXIV.—Compare Part I. Fab. LIX. The epimyths present the chief difference between the two.

FAB. XXVIII.—Compare the epimyth of this fable, which has a political end in view, with Fable 39, Part I. v. 3, 4.

FAB. XXXII.—There is no prose version extant of this singular fable. But it may be compared with Babr. Part I. Fab. 57. and Part II. 52, with which it, in parts, corresponds. The three concluding verses seem hopelessly corrupt, and defy translation.

FAB. XXXVII.—Cf. Fab. XII. p. 1, and Fab. XC. Part II. and see Note on the former.

FAB. XXXIX.—Horace, Epist. I. x. 34. Aristot. Rhet. II. 20.

FAB. XLI. 6.—Pliny, in his Natural History, x. 24, says of the cock, "that it is an object of terror even to lions, the noblest of the brute kind." The elephant seems to be very sensitive of the attacks of insects, frequently rolling itself in mud, contracting his skin, and so crushing them between its wrinkles, or gathering boughs with his trunk to brush them away, or, if these artifices fail, collecting dust with his trunk, and strewing it over the most sensible parts of his body. See Encycl. Britann. Art. Mammalia, vol. 12, pp. 469, 70.

FAB. XLII.—Compare Fab. LXV. in Part I. and LXXXV. Part II. Avianus, Fab. 15, says, "Threiciam volucrem fertur Junonius ales," &c., and Ælian notes that the crane migrates in the autumn to Libya and Ægypt, N. A. II. 1, III. 13. Compare Aristoph. Aves. 710. The epimyth here and at Fable LXV. in the first part are very similar.

FAB. LI.—Compare CXXVIII. in Part I.

FAB. LII.—Compare above, Fab. XXXI. Part II.

FAB. LIII. LIV.—Compare with these respectively, Fragm. I. in Part I. and Fable CXXV. in Part I. The translation is made up of a comparison of both. The Maltese dog is mentioned by Aristot. H. A. X. 6 ; Probl. X. 12.

FAB. LIX.—In the application of the fable of the Belly and its Members, as related by Shakespeare, (Coriolanus, Act I. Scene 1,) Menenius calls one of the citizens, "the great toe of the assembly,"

" For that being one of the lowest, basest, poorest,
Of this most wise rebellion, thou goest forward."

The fables are wholly dissimilar in purpose, but these words of Shakespeare are a parallel to the description of the tail in this fable of Babrius.

FAB. LXIV.—Simonides of Amorgos, in his poem περὶ γυναικῶν, represents Jove as having formed women out of brutes, availing himself of the nature of each, *e.g.* the craft of the fox, or the cleverness of the ape, in moulding the nature and character of each woman. For Prometheus, and his part in the fable, Cf. Horace, Od. I. xvi. 13 "Fertur Prometheus," &c. Fulgent, Mythol. III. De Peleo, and see Ovid Met. I. 82—8. See also above, Part I. Fab. LXVI. note.

FAB. LXVII.—The reading ξηρὴν instead of θήρην in v. 14 has been adopted for translation.

FAB. LXXI.—See note in Kitto's Bible on Psalm lii. 8, respecting the greenness and long life of the olive tree.

FAB. LXXII.—Avianus (Fab. 40) has a version of this fable, the concluding lines of which are,—

Vade, ait, et pictæ nimium confide figuræ,
  Dum mihi consilium pulchrius esse queat,
Miremurque magis quos munera mentis adornant,
  Quam qui corporeis enituere bonis.

FAB. LXXIII.—Compare Aristotle, Rhet. II. 20, where, however, a demagogue, not a rich man, is represented as on his trial. Tiberius used this fable, a little altered, as a reason for not often changing governors of provinces, or appointing successors, unless in case of a governor's death. See Whiston's Josephus, Antiq. Jews, Book XVIII. c. vi. note 5.

FAB. LXXVIII.—Compare with this fable, illustrative of the force of nature, Part I. Fab. XXXII. It is given also by Lucian; Piscator, c. 36, who likewise tells it of a king of Egypt. See also Lucian's Apology, c. v. where the monkeys are said to have been the property of Cleopatra.

FAB. LXXX.—See Aristot. H. A. IX. 40. Pliny, H. A. XI. c. 17. Nicander Theriaca, v. 809. Virg. Georg. IV. 236, and Servius's note there.

FAB. LXXXI.—Compare the story of Atys and Adrastus, Herodot. I. 34—45.

FAB. LXXXIV.—Sir G. C. Lewis suggests the omission of

v. 2 in the text of this fable, and, for ὠκύπους, reading Ἵππευεν in the end of v. 1.

F̲AB̲. LXXXVI.—This fable is narrated nearly word for word by Sylla, in a speech recorded in Appian's Civil Wars, Book I. p. 413. Steph. q. v.

F̲AB̲. XC.—Compare with this fable, Fab. XII. Part 1. According to Homer, Od. XIX. 517—23, Zethus, king of Thebes, married Aedon, daughter of Pandareus, and Itylus was the offspring of this union. She slew her son in mistake for the eldest child of Niobe, her husband's brother's wife. Sir G. C. Lewis suggests reading μητρὸς or Πρόκνης at the end of v. 42, for Ζήθου, and referring the whole, as is most natural, to the tragical tale of Tereus and Procne. Itylus was slain by the sword of Aedon, not of Zethus.

F̲AB̲. XCV.—For the proverb περὶ ὄνου σκιᾶς, see Lucian. Hermotim 71; Aristoph. Vesp. 191, and the Scholiast there, who says that the fable was used by Menander, in one of his plays; and by Demosthenes, see Orat. De Pace, p. 63, notes, and Plat. Phædr. p. 203, and the notes of Ast and others. It seems, in all these passages, that the proverb refers to contentions about matters of the very slightest moment.

FINIS.